THE QUILT

"The magical quilt is a powerful symbol of a deeper reality. It is like the First Matter of the alchemists or the view quantum physicists have of matter. It changes its physical properties to reflect the state of consciousness of the observer."
- Dennis William Hauck, alchemist, teacher, and author of *The Emerald Tablet* and *The Sorcerer's Stone*

"THE QUILT is not so much a novel as a parable. It's as if The Celestine Prophecy met The Picture of Dorian Gray, only this picture of the quilt - just keeps getting better and better."
- Mary K. Greer, Tarot teacher, author of *Who Are You in the Tarot?*

"An adventurous celebration of life's mysteries and the Soul's longings to find its way home. THE QUILT is a Castaneda-like tale, but told through a woman's heart and hard-earned wisdom."
- Steve Gross, writer

"Quite intriguing. I was interested to see how Alex transformed. Thanks to the visual writing style, I can see this story as a film unfolding."
- Laura Paulsen, filmmaker

"What a beautiful story! It made me cry. It's Beauty and the Beast meets the Art of Dreaming; I love it. Alex is both an inspirational heroine and a very personable character. She feels very real to me. I wanted to keep reading the story to find out what happens, and at the same time go slowly and savor Alex's transformations."
- Elena Powell, musician, artist

THE QUILT

A Woman's Spiritual Journey to Power

Nanci Shanderá, Ph.D.

THE QUILT
A Woman's Spiritual Journey to Power

Published by ShadowWolf Press
578 Sutton Way #395
Grass Valley, CA 95945
www.EarthSpiritCenter.com

This book is a work of fiction. Names, characters, places, and
incidents are products of the author's imagination or are used
fictitiously. Any resemblance to actual events or locales or
persons, living or dead, is entirely coincidental.

ISBN 978-0615731858

Cover Illustration: Valerie Kack, Ph.D.

Dedicated to all who seek

ACKNOWLEDGMENTS

I wish to thank my daughter, Ashley, for all her help. I could never have birthed this book by myself!

Additional thanks to Dr. Valerie Kack for her gorgeous cover art, and all my students through the years who have taught me so much.

And, as always, unending gratitude to my beloved teacher, Brugh Joy, M.D.

AUTHOR'S NOTE:

The characters and adventures in this novel are fictional, though drawn from personal experiences that reflect processes in the classic "Hero's Journey," a potent metaphor for the process of spiritual transformation. Most of us in the modern world have lost touch with the richness of myth and rites of passage, whose purpose was and is to guide spiritual seekers in their quest for enlightenment and wholeness. This story is intended to be a symbolic foundation that may support anyone on the spiritual pathway. It is meant to transform perceptions of what is required to gain self-realization, and the necessity of embracing the more challenging elements of the transformational process. There is no pathway consisting entirely of light - just as we need night to balance the day, we must reevaluate commonly held beliefs about the dark and learn to balance it with the light. The heroine in this work is a composite woman. She was created from the substance of my personal experiences as well as those of my students through the years. Her character is meant to illustrate her limitations and her inability to access them until she is thrust into otherworldly, life changing experiences. She is a workaholic, and comes from a dysfunctional family whose fears she passes down to her daughter. She feels victimized and powerless, she doesn't trust others, and is terrified to look inside herself in order to see who she truly might be. As she is led by two extraordinary teachers to explore deeper levels of herself, she begins to realize the power and light that emanate from within her. She faces, then transforms lifelong challenges, attitudes, and limitations that had always prevented her from awakening to her spiritual authenticity.

Joseph Campbell's classic, *Hero With A Thousand Faces*, and Maureen Murdock's *The Heroine's Journey*, provide further information about the experiences described in *The Quilt*. If you are exploring your own spiritual transformation, I highly recommend these books.

Certainly, I hope to entertain you as you read, but to also plant a seed that grows within you and heals beliefs in dualities of all kinds, particularly the one that says the world of imagination, dreams and myth are not real and therefore not to be taken seriously. It has been my experience that the integration of ordinary and non-ordinary realities expands perception of and gives great meaning to our place and purpose in life. Symbology, metaphor and myth have held the world together for centuries. The power of these gifts holds the potential of holding it together for our future.

I sincerely hope that this story provides support, assistance and inspiration for all who have made the decision to live authentically. I welcome comments and questions from readers who can contact me at www.EarthSpiritCenter.com.

Many blessings!

CHAPTER 1

She ran, fighting for more breath and screaming at her long legs to move faster over the rocky terrain. She didn't dare look back at the slavering, panting, grunting beast that was trailing her. Choking for more air, she knew she must somehow reach safety. What did the beast want? Why was she being pursued? She only knew her life depended on outrunning the ferocious beast. Her fear compounded as she imagined what the creature must look like. She couldn't think of that now. Her heart pounded in her chest until she thought it might burst. Her burning legs began to cramp. She began crying aloud for them not to stop, to keep going. Suddenly, she stumbled. She scrambled to pull herself up again and resumed her frantic pace. She could feel the hot, fetid breath of the beast on her back as she lost the advantage of distance between them. She knew if she fell again, the creature would have her. She saw ahead of her a clearing in the forest and a rise in the ground. She hoped it meant a river so she could dive in and elude her pursuer. Perhaps the beast couldn't swim. She pushed for more speed and determined that she would run up and leap over the rise in hopes that the river would appear. As she lengthened her stride up the hill, her fatigue diminished and every bit of her focus was on getting over the ridge. She didn't see the cliff's edge until it was almost too late. She braked by grabbing onto a small thorn bush. She slid to the ground, her left leg dangling precariously over the edge. She was vaguely aware that her sandal had fallen into the abyss. The thorns pierced her hands and ripped at the flesh. Her legs were torn and bloody from her violent halt. Exhaustion and shock left her unprepared for the huge, dark shadow that loomed over her. The beast was upon her in an instant. It ripped at her scalp with its talons and snatched at her face with its slavering teeth. Its panting increased as it tore into her defenseless body, ripping her arms from their sockets, tearing at her legs until they became useless, limp appendages. She tried to scream with the pain, but could not because her throat had been torn away. As she sank into unconsciousness....

Alex Wilder awoke, panting, sweating and terrified, making whimpering sounds as she groped at her shaking body to make sure it was still intact. Her mind reeled, stunned at how deeply the dream had affected her.

She rose, trembling, and stumbled into the bathroom, shoving her disheveled, chestnut-colored hair out of her eyes. As she poured a tumbler of cool water, she peered into her deep brown eyes in the mirror for some sense of reality but she only saw intense terror and bewilderment. Dark markings like bruises encircled them. She shook her head to clear it, leaning over the sink in case she should vomit, and sipped her water slowly to get her bearings. Shreds of memory began to arise, taking her back into the horror. She pushed herself firmly away from the sink and stepped resolutely back into the bedroom.

This is ridiculous. It was only a nightmare. Probably the pizza I had before bed. I'll just get ready for work...in fact, I'll go in early so I can get my mind off that stupid dream. No sense in belaboring an overblown figment of my imagination.

She teased herself into a false sense of relief and began preparing for her shower. She was annoyed that her favorite classical radio station was playing Stravinsky's *Rite of Spring*. The piece filled her with so much anxiety that she slapped the switch to turn it off. Looking back into the mirror, she rubbed impatiently at the smudged eye shadow beneath her eyes and saw terror looking back at her.

She slammed her hand down hard on the counter and cried, "No! This is not going to get to me!"

The sound of her husky voice startled her and Alex sank onto the light blue carpet and dizzily realized how deeply the dream had affected her. She was glad Rosie, her lively seven-year-old daughter, was staying with her father for the summer so she wouldn't be upset by Alex's bizarre mood.

Running her fingers through her shoulder-length mop of hair, Alex sat in silence for some time before she pulled herself up to stand. She had a foreboding sense that her experience could not be disregarded as merely an annoying product of a heavy meal the night before.

She adjusted the hot water faucet in the tiled shower stall and stepped, heavy-footed, into the sharp spray of steaming water.

CHAPTER 2

Alex had intended to slip into her office without having to talk to anyone. She planned to closet herself behind a closed door and attack her usual mountain of paperwork. But the typical routine at the Billings Agency had always included the "good mornings" and "how are yous" that now she couldn't avoid. This morning, she merely nodded impatiently as her coworkers, who were waiting for the coffee machine to spit out its dark and aromatic brew, faced her with greetings.

Eileen, Alex's secretary, sensing another stressful day both for and with her boss, attempted as she always did, to assist Alex. "Would you like some coffee, Ms. Wilder?"

Alex, in desperation to avoid all human contact, didn't answer and rushed into her office. She pushed the door to close it, but her hand slipped and it crashed shut behind her, the noise reverberating throughout the entire office. She moaned to herself, knowing what the reaction of the others in the hall would be to what they would interpret as one of her displays of hot temper.

She shrugged it off and removed her coat. As she hung it on the wooden rack by the door, she began to feel dizzy. As she grabbed the edge of her large oak desk to prevent a fall, the dream of that morning flashed before her mind's eye.

Pulling over a deeply upholstered chair, she dropped into it and shook her head, holding it in her hands and resting her elbows on the desktop.

"No, this is not going to affect me. I have too much to do," she whispered to herself, a sob catching in her throat.

Pulling herself out of the chair, she looked around for a restorative cup of coffee, then cursed aloud at not having taken Eileen up on her offer. She longed for a hot drink and the shock of caffeine, but pride and lack of nerve prevented her from buzzing Eileen.

Settling for bottled water, Alex sat in the chair behind her desk and settled down to the stack of correspondence she had been neglecting for the past few days. One letter was from a Jim Buckingham, one of her firm's clients.

"Ugh, what does *he* want?" she muttered. This man had ideas that she considered naive and she had always wondered why he even bothered to hire a large advertising firm to assist him in getting his message out. "Hmph, he should stick to business instead of this cheesy stuff he's into." She sniffed and tossed his letter into a "to do later" pile.

Jim Buckingham's expansive hardware and landscape gardening business had recently been through a major restructuring from one that had been a successful and hugely lucrative enterprise, to one that now encompassed egalitarian and profit-sharing principles, one that he said empowered every employee. Alex frowned upon such foolish ideas and believed he had signed his business' own death warrant the moment he had succumbed to these "New Agey" ideas.

As she continued working, her need for caffeine overrode her pride and she hailed Eileen over the intercom to bring her a cup of coffee - black. "And make sure it's hot this time," she added imperiously.

As Eileen rushed to the coffee machine, her knees felt like water. She poured the steaming liquid into a styrofoam cup with one hand as she adjusted her blond, curly hair with the other. She hated working for Alex Wilder but was too insecure in her abilities to search for work elsewhere. She had worked for Alex's predecessor, who had been an older and extremely kind woman. She had cried at Mrs. Reed's retirement party, but didn't realize at the time the grief she would feel daily with her new boss. Everyone at Billings commiserated with Eileen and, just like Eileen, gave Alex a wide berth. Even the top executives, although respecting Alex's ability to land large accounts in record time, made sure they had no more contact with her than what was absolutely necessary.

Alex Wilder was not well liked.

CHAPTER 3

As she battled traffic on her way home, Alex worried that she might have another chapter of the dream from that morning. But as the week went by, one night blended uneventfully into the next until she successfully pushed the horrors of the dream out of her conscious mind.

A few weeks later, Alex sat at her dark oak desk, speaking to a client on the telephone. Eileen cautiously entered the office, bending low as she placed some papers on Alex's desk.

Annoyed, Alex waved Eileen out, but Eileen, misunderstanding, only moved closer, awaiting her presumed task.

Covering the mouthpiece, Alex exploded, "Get out! And stop coming in here when my door is closed!"

Eileen's blue eyes flashed in shock, then filled with tears. She turned quickly and exited, closing the door behind her.

"Sorry," Alex said to her client. "The help around here is really...Hello? Mr. Stanger? Are you there?"

She held the receiver away from her ear and stared at it, then smashed it down in its cradle.

"Rude, rude, rude. Why are people so rude!" she exclaimed.

For the rest of the day, no one entered her office and her phone didn't ring. She accepted this respite as proof of her success as a manager, thinking that Eileen had finally gotten the message.

Walking down the hall at the end of the day, briefcase in one hand, stacks of files and car keys in the other, Alex's mind was on grabbing a chicken salad at the deli around the corner from the parking garage before going home. She planned to do a quick workout on one of her exercise DVDs, and then get to work on two new accounts she wanted to nail. She was startled out of her reverie by the voice of her boss, Ralph Billings.

"Alex. Could I have a word with you for a moment please?"

"Certainly, Mr. Billings," Alex said as she stepped into his spacious office. She looked around as if hoping to see a more orderly and businesslike environment than the one she always saw. As usual, she was disappointed. Piles of papers were scattered, helter-skelter, on each available surface. She sighed as she settled her slim body into a chair that was, by her estimation, too soft. *Hmph. Should be in a living room, not in an office.*

"Alex, I've been increasingly concerned about you," Mr. Billings began, loosening his striped tie. Ralph Billings was a middle-aged African-American man who truly loved his work, particularly the people he worked with. Most all of his employees appreciated what he tried to do to create a positive work environment. Alex, on the other hand, hadn't a clue as to what the man's deep, feeling-level intentions were. She merely thought of him as ordinary and a bit too "wishy-washy" when it came to running the business. She had always considered herself next in line when Mr. Billings retired and she had detailed plans for dramatic changes. She believed the people who worked there could choose to adhere to them or merely quit, unless they, like Eileen, were on Alex's "To Fire" list.

"Whatever for?" she said, answering his expression of concern, cutting him off with a laugh that did not ring true. She struggled to affect a confidence she didn't feel by crossing her legs and leaning her chin on one fist. *What now?* she thought, feeling annoyed at what she perceived as a waste of time.

"Well," he continued, leaning toward her across his cluttered desk. "It's come to my attention that you've been...well, shall we say...less than relaxed lately."

Alex's face tightened. "And just who brought this silliness to your attention?" Her body followed her face by straightening into a rigid defensive posture.

"It doesn't matter who, Alex. I've noticed it myself."

"Noticed what?" she asked, trying to readjust her legs so she looked casual and unaffected. She was vaguely aware of an increasingly tight band of tension across her forehead.

"I think you need to take some time off, Alex. To rest. To get your bearings."

"That's utter nonsense," she said, brushing nonexistent lint from her skirt. Then, fearing she was offending him, "I don't know what people have been telling you but if they spent more time working as I do and less time around the coffee maker, they wouldn't have time to complain about me - or anything else for that matter. Mr. Billings, I believe you've been listening to a bunch of malcontents. They're envious of anyone who's really making it."

Having said her piece, she settled, satisfied, back into the chair, this time grateful it was so comfortable. She started to place her files onto the table next to her, but seeing it was already full of papers, she put them on the floor and folded her hands in her lap, satisfied she had cleared herself of the charges against her. She then focused on trying to will the headache away.

"I'm truly sorry, but I don't agree, Alex. As I said, I think you should take some time off," Mr. Billings said. His face was filled with solicitude.

"That's impossible. I have two new accounts that..."

Mr. Billings stood up and interrupted her. "Alex, you're not hearing what I'm saying. I'm not *asking* you to take some time off. I'm *telling* you."

Alex blinked at the firmness in his voice. She watched him as he leaned down against his curled fists on the desk and she knew he meant what he said.

She found she had no words to counter what he had just told her.

As she tried to regain her composure and gather her bag, keys and files from the floor, she narrowed her eyes at him.

"And just how much 'time off' are you 'recommending'?" she asked, barely disguising her bitterness.

"As much as you need, Alex. As much as you need."

CHAPTER 4

The gently winding mountain road spun past Alex as she drove, her head leaning wearily on her hand, her arm crooked on the open window of her late model, green Acura sedan. She was relieved to be free of what she saw as paranoia in her office. *They can just cool their heels for a while. Without me around they'll see how invaluable I am.* She laughed ironically to herself.

She had phoned her former husband, David, who told her their daughter Rosie was having a wonderful time at day camp so she probably wouldn't miss her mother's nightly calls for a while. She didn't know whether to feel reassured by that or not. She worried about Rosie whenever she was away. David was a good father but his ideas about child raising were too permissive for her liking. She was relieved he hadn't pressed her for details about why she was taking an unplanned vacation.

She was in a hurry to leave the bustle of the city but had no particular destination. Early morning mountain smells of pine and the sweet calls of birds soothed her senses like a balm before she became aware that she had begun to relax. She decreased her speed and felt hopeful that the day would erase the lunacy of her last day at work. She shifted her position in the tan leather seat, appreciating its softness as she pushed her back tightly up against it, while expanding her chest and taking a deep, refreshing breath. Surprised, she heard her throat expel a sigh of relief and then a giggle. She drove on with new determination to enjoy the next few days as a holiday.

Feeling hungry, she pulled into a dusty parking lot at an old truck stop cafe, and chuckled to herself that she would be considering eating at such a place. But she emerged from her car, strode confidently toward the diner, and made plans to order something light.

Can't ever be too careful about food in these places. That must have been the message of that awful nightmare. I need to start taking better care of myself. Even though weeks had passed since she had the dream, she was still trying to avoid its irksome residue.

Alex entered the dimly lit diner and sat down at the counter on a swivel chair that that had several poorly repaired tears in its red Naugahyde seat. She pulled a paper napkin out of its holder and wiped down the counter before her, then warily picked up a greasy menu and looked at the selections. She opted for a cup of chicken noodle soup and a side of dry rye toast. As the man behind the counter appeared, she spoke her order aloud without looking up.

"Got traveler's stomach?" asked the tall man, who wore a cook's cap that looked as though it had survived too many ineffective attempts at washing. He was chewing gum loudly and looked bored. His face was heavily pockmarked and bore a day-old smattering of beard.

She looked up, startled out of her reveries, and muttered, "Oh, uh, no. The soup and toast will be fine." She perceived the man as being far too personal and was annoyed by his impertinence.

She adjusted her tailored grey jacket and defensively straightened her posture on the seat. The man gave her a look that revealed his feelings about uppity women and returned to the kitchen to prepare the food, popping his gum as he disappeared behind the squeaky swinging door.

As she waited, she looked about the place. She was the only customer and it was comforting not to be bothered by others. The cafe looked like it was built around 1930 with not much improvement made since then. Alex noticed some peeling paint over the entrance and guessed any remodeling efforts had involved merely painting over grease-stained walls.

In her peripheral vision, Alex saw movement outside the window and pivoted the swivel seat for a better view. An older model car had stopped in front of the cafe, its engine still running. There was nothing remarkable about the scene so she began to turn her seat around again but halted when she noticed a man, whose long dark hair was tied back in a ponytail, emerge from the rust-flecked car. There was something about him that riveted her attention. Alex continued watching as he leaned in to say something to the woman in the driver's seat, whose mass of hair was long, dark and wavy. Alex saw what she thought was a younger, brown-haired woman in the back seat but she couldn't get a good view to be sure.

The man walked away with long strides and she assumed the woman would drive off. But the engine continued to idle and the driver made no move. Alex had a strange feeling that time was expanding and slowing at the same time, as if minutes were hours. Suddenly, the dark-haired man appeared again and began to open the passenger door. With his hand resting on the doorframe, he turned his face slowly toward the cafe window and looked piercingly into Alex's eyes. She was shocked and her body jolted. Although she didn't see his lips moving, she swore she heard a powerful voice in her ear asking, "Are you paying attention?"

At that, the man stepped into the car and the woman accelerated, leaving a cloud of dust and pebbles as the tires scrambled for traction. Alex strained to see the passenger in the back seat but she seemed to have disappeared.

Shocked to her core, Alex continued to stare out of the grime-streaked window. She felt as rattled as if she had been physically struck. The dust from the car cleared and everything became eerily still. She was vaguely aware that even the sounds from the kitchen had diminished.

Suddenly, she felt herself expanding into a kind of hyper-awareness where she felt herself in two realities at once. Part of her was sitting in the diner but another part was clearly somewhere else. Giddiness overtook her even while her mind fought for a logical explanation. Curiously, she was not afraid and even yielded to her new state of mind with its strange perceptions. Her body felt different, lighter, yet more connected to the ground. She slid off her stool and made her way over to the window, pressing her fingertips gently against the cool glass, now unconcerned with its oily surface. She strained to see down the road in the direction the rusty car had gone.

Suddenly, she felt an exhilarating feeling of expansion rising in her chest, followed by a laugh that bubbled forth from deep within her.

Startled by her outburst, Alex dropped back abruptly into her ordinary reality. Knees shaking, she sank weakly into a wooden chair by the window and attempted to gather her thoughts. She looked down at her clothes and touched her face lightly. She flinched when the gum-popping cook appeared.

"D'ya want yer soup here or t'the counter?" He was balancing a cracked bowl of chicken noodle soup and a plate of toast in one hand.

"Who were those people?" she asked, ignoring his question.

"What?" The gum popped again.

"The ones in that car. That man and woman."

Squinting his eyes, the cook looked at her suspiciously, sizing her up.

"Look, Lady, there ain't been nobody past here since you drove up. I know, cuz I can see out t'the lot even when I'm doin' the cookin' in the kitchen. See?" He motioned with his arm toward the large window that opened from the kitchen to the dining room.

Alex, sensing his distrust, decided against arguing her point. *He's obviously lying.* But his motivation for doing so eluded her. As the man shifted his weight, waiting for an answer to his question about the food, she caught a glimpse of herself in a mirror on the wall behind him. Behind her left shoulder was a hazy image of the couple in the car. They were standing there smiling at her.

"My god!" she exclaimed aloud, startling the cook as well as herself. She saw his increasing agitation, so she rose from her chair, grabbed a couple of bills from her black leather purse and pushed them into his large, beefy hand.

Stumbling out of the cafe, Alex leaned on the side of her car for several moments, taking in large gulps of the crisp mountain air to clear her now throbbing head.

She opened the driver side door and sat down on the soft seat, fumbling with the keys. She selected one and poked it into the ignition slot but when she tried to start the engine, the key would not turn. She tried forcing it, but it stubbornly refused to engage. She yanked the key out and realized that it was the key to the trunk. She made another selection and this time the engine started with a loud roar as she gunned the accelerator pedal.

The cook, who was still holding her bowl of soup and plate of toast, just stared after her.

"City folks. They're all nuts!" He returned to the kitchen, shaking his head, stuffing the money into his pocket, and popping his gum two times in succession.

CHAPTER 5

As she raced along the winding two-lane highway, Alex was terrified of what she suspected might be happening to her. She hastily reviewed her family's history, exploring her lifelong suspicion of genetic mental illness. Although she could think of no medically diagnosed pathologies, she knew her relatives had never sought the psychological help that could have confirmed such conditions.

Well, there's always a first time. Now, worry joined with her rising panic.

A neatly painted roadside sign caught her attention and she slowed to read it. "Kozee Kottages...1 mile on Left...Doubles...Singles." The fast approaching dusk made the decision for her and when she reached the motel, she rolled into the gravel lot by the sign that said, "Office. Please ring bell for service."

After checking in, Alex thanked the proprietor who carried her heavy suitcase to her room. He was elderly but fit, and had a nice smile. He and his silver-haired wife had insisted upon assuring her their beds were vermin-free and the room was safe and quiet. The woman had told her that there was even a little stream behind her little log cabin that was nice to listen to at night if she kept the window open.

Alex tried to push a tip into the man's hand but he refused it, telling her that while she was here, this was her home. She just stared at him, not fully comprehending his generosity, and muttered her thanks.

As he left, closing the door behind him, Alex looked around the small, cozy room and sank down onto the soft bed. Its creaking seemed somehow soothing to her. She noticed the spread was actually a handmade, rainbow-colored quilt. *Probably the wife's handiwork.* She ran her hand over the slightly faded but intricate patterns, looked around and decided this was indeed a safe place. She let out a tired sigh and pulled her suitcase up onto the bed.

When she finished her unpacking, she walked the few hundred yards back to the office to tell the proprietors she had decided to stay for more than just the one night. They seemed delighted with her decision. She asked the location of nearby restaurants but recoiled when they mentioned the cafe where she had had her strange experiences earlier. She relaxed when they pointed in the opposite direction, assuring her that there were several other decent eating establishments in the nearby town. They said there was even a resort in the mountains that boasted a first-class dining room should she want to make the short drive. She thanked them and wandered out onto the well-manicured property to get her bearings.

Alex noticed that the foothills, under which the cabins were nestled, were dusty rose in color, caressed by the setting sun. Nature's beauty soothed her and she decided to walk behind her cabin to look for the stream the old woman had mentioned.

As she approached, the sound of water gushing over rocks filled her with pleasure and she quickened her steps. At the water's edge, Alex bent to allow the water to wash over her hand. Its iciness refreshed her and she found a nearby rock where she sat down, pulled off her shoes and stockings, and dangled her feet in the stream, not caring how cold it was. It ignited a calming feeling within her that she couldn't quite identify. The sensation of water rushing over her feet relaxed her. She found herself wondering about the river in the nightmare and the one in which she was now wriggling her toes gleefully. She scoffed at the idea, determining there was no connection whatsoever. A sense of deep peace washed over her and she felt a pleasing tingling moving up her spine. She recalled having had a similar sensation recently at a symphonic concert. She remembered how powerful the music was and how it had seemed to carry her into another world.

CHAPTER 6

Awakening the next morning, Alex stretched languidly. She was surprised that her muscles were stiff and sore, but didn't think much about it because the gurgling sound of the stream outside her window drew her once more into a sense of peace. She had almost forgotten the events of the preceding day and felt glad now that she had some time away from work. Again, she convinced herself that the experiences at the cafe had only indicated how much she had needed a break.

"Work-related stress. Maybe Billings was right," she said aloud, as she arose from the bed, mindlessly smoothing and patting the quilted spread.

She noticed the primitive pattern of the shapes and colors on the quilt and wondered whether it actually was the handiwork of the proprietor's wife or someone else. She leaned closer to study the motif. Why this fascinated her she had no idea. She had never before been even the slightest bit interested in handicrafts. Now she caught herself examining the multi-colored piece with intense curiosity.

She bolted upright when she heard a rapping at the door. She opened it carefully, squinting her dark brown eyes against the bright sun. It was the old man, wearing a ragged straw cowboy hat and smiling at her.

"My wife and I are going down the road to her sister's for the day and just wondered if you needed anything before we leave."

She was relieved and uncharacteristically grateful for the attention. She opened the door wide.

"Oh, thanks for your concern but I don't need a thing. I think I'll do a little hiking up into the hills."

"Well, then, you have a good day, Miss. But you be careful of those mountains. Wear your lug soles and take plenty of water and some matches. Just so's you'll be safe if you get lost." He chuckled, tipped his hat to her, and stepped off the porch.

As she closed the door, Alex muttered to herself that he hadn't needed to plant the seed of concern about her well-being. She didn't want something else to worry about. She vowed to stay on the trail and that would take care of any possibility of trouble. She laughed out loud at the ridiculous idea of getting lost.

She took a long, leisurely shower, then dressed in a pair of pressed jeans and a crisp white blouse. She tied a windbreaker around her shoulders and packed a small knapsack with an apple and a protein bar, remembering to include a book of matches and the bottle of water she always kept in her car. She smiled again at the old man's concern, but welcomed the supplies anyway. She checked around the room as she opened the door to leave, and wondered why, after closing it behind her, she felt uneasy. She had carefully locked her valuables in her car and believed there was no reason for apprehension.

Alex found the hiking trail easily and began the climb upward. The wind whipped her long hair and she wished she had brought a bandana or, better yet, a hat. The sun beat down and began to burn her scalp. Bushes that bordered the narrow trail up the mountainside scratched her uncovered arms. She pulled the windbreaker on but invisible flying insects still succeeded in biting her at irritating intervals. She spent much of her time swatting at them.

Several times she thought of returning to the cabin, but she tossed the idea off as just a silly fear induced by the old man's warning. She truly wanted to reach the top of the ridge because it looked so cool and inviting with all its tall pines and lush greenery. She admitted to herself that she had miscalculated the distance to the ridge, but justified her persistence in continuing by telling herself it was only a little further.

Finally reaching the crest, Alex felt expended and a bit giddy at her triumph. She looked back down the trail and was able to make out the cabins, now in miniature relief against the blue, cloud-bedecked sky. She was satisfied with her feat and sat with her back against a large aromatic pine, whose reddish-brown bark was ragged and scratched. It made a comfortable backrest and she closed her eyes, feeling at peace. Even the biting bugs had ceased their attacks.

She took a swallow of water and, as she rested, Alex considered the range of emotions she had experienced the last few days. It led her to question the predictability of her life: Drop Rosie off at school, drive to work, see clients, go to meetings, promote the firm, stay late, pick up Rosie at the sitter's, help her daughter with homework, put her to bed, and fall into bed herself. Not much of a social life since she took on the assistant directorship of the advertising agency. But she had believed it was worth it. It gave her the step forward she had worked feverishly hard to gain. She had enjoyed the feelings of accomplishment that seemed to her to be a guarantee that her future was secure. But she was vaguely aware now, resting against the tree in this new environment, that her work filled her life so completely that she wouldn't have face her deep fears of being alone.

Her eyes flashed open. *Alone! Me? That's nonsense. I'm with people all day long.*

She laid her head back against the tree and tried to relax once more. The silence of the forest amplified her attempted rationalizations. Defeated, she opened her eyes once more and she recognized the reality of her loneliness, not only here on the mountainside, but in the rest of her life as well. She wrapped her arms around her knees and stared up at the sky. She felt hot tears gathering in the corners of her eyes. Annoyed, she brushed them away, but more formed in their place until finally, she could fight them no longer and Alex succumbed to sobs.

After a while, she lifted her head and was dismayed by the change in the light. The sun was going down and she had no idea how time had eluded her. She felt a rising sense of panic and quickly gathered her pack, throwing her windbreaker around her shoulders and tying the sleeves in front. She stumbled rapidly down the hill, believing herself to be on the same trail she had used earlier.

In her rush, she failed to notice that the trail that brought her up the mountain was one graced with scrubby vegetation. Now, she was groping through a stand of tall pines. She slowed to get her bearings but, not really knowing what her bearings were, continued on. She thrashed through a thick bed of needles, broken branches, and fallen trunks, which were hollowed by time and insect invasion.

"Damn!" she said, finally realizing she was lost and the old man's prediction had come true.

Alex turned toward each of what she guessed might be the cardinal directions, hoping for a sense of something that might guide her. Her heart sank when all four positions looked the same. The forest had become very dark, the sky blocked by a crazy tangle of branches.

She sank down on the soft, spongy forest floor. She knew crying would do nothing to help her calculate her way out of this predicament. But she also knew she was facing the very real possibility of having to spend the night alone in this frightening place. The light that remained was creating shadows that took on ominous potentials for danger. She felt her heart racing and she knew she must calm down so she could make some rational decisions.

Even in the failing light, she could see the scratchings on the trees and suddenly realized, with a sickening, sinking feeling in her stomach, that the slash marks may well indicate the presence of bears.

She gasped aloud and leapt up. She raced through the thick forest, oblivious of the branches that snatched at her sleeves and tore her windbreaker from her shoulders. She thought she heard something chasing her and dizzily spun around, only to slam her head roughly into an overhanging limb. She sank to her knees, holding her head in her hands. Tears burst forth and she wailed, rocking herself on her knees.

"Why is this happening to me?" Alex pleaded angrily. "What did I do to deserve this?"

CHAPTER 7

Sobbing wracked her until her energy was depleted. Dirt and tears stained her face into a mask of black, grey, and reddish-brown. Sleep overtook her and Alex surrendered to it.

Some time later, she was awakened by a gentle nudging on her side. Alex was startled to consciousness by the sight of a reddish-hued, medium-sized bear, who was sniffing and pawing at her ragged clothes. She gasped and began to cautiously pull herself away when she heard a deep voice.

"He will not hurt you."

She spun around in the direction of the sound and saw a man's face, darkened by the shadows in the forest. Alex felt a strange recognition. The man wore a red Pendleton shirt, buttoned at the neck and wrists. His long hair was smoky gray and slightly wavy. The skin on his face was weathered and leathery, but gave no clue of his age. She studied him as he silently waited for her response.

Alex pulled herself to a sitting position and began brushing her clothes furiously, as if their condition mattered. She heard him chuckling quietly and when she looked up, she thought his eyes were twinkling.

"Where am I? What is happening here?" she asked, bewildered.

Seeming not to respond, the man began to build a fire inside a ring of rocks, which she had not noticed before. She thought nothing of it, however, because the fire began warming her chilled body and she leaned forward to relieve her frozen hands.

As she reached toward the ring of fire, the man suddenly leapt at her and forced her hands into the flames. She screamed and tried frantically to wrench her hands free.

"Stop struggling," he warned her.

Alex looked incredulously at the madman for what seemed to be a very long time. When she realized that her hands were still in the flames and were not burning, she started to pull them away from him again. But to her surprise, he was no longer holding her hands in the fire. She was holding them there on her own accord and what she saw in them riveted her attention. Bursting forth from her palms were rainbow-colored flames, but rather than burning hot, they were warm and electric, and radiated skyward.

"Pull your hands out of the fire," the man instructed softly.

She hesitated, entranced by the beauty of the flames.

"Do as I say." His voice was firm, but gentle.

Unsure whether or not she should follow his bidding, Alex reluctantly removed her hands from the fire. She was shocked when she saw that they continued to emit the rainbow flames. She peered, wide-eyed, into her palms, watching how the intensity of the flames changed as her thoughts changed from fear to fascination. She was mesmerized.

The man's deep voice jolted her out of her reverie. "This has been shown to you to teach you of the work you will do."

She turned, confused, but he was gone. As she looked up, all she saw was the red bear lumbering off into the woods. As she looked down, the flames in her hands had faded.

Then all Alex was aware of was the soft whisper of the wind in the pines and that she was filled with awe.

CHAPTER 8

Alex awoke to the twittering and fluttering of birds and the pungent smell of pine. She looked up and saw the thick blanket of treetops and heard the breeze ruffling the branches. To her relief, light was filtering through the forest and she pulled herself up to a sitting position. She felt a large bump on her head, where it had hit the tree.

She was at a loss to understand how she had lasted through the night. She had been so sure that a bear would attack her. She had vague feelings of having had some kind of interaction with one, but dismissed them as unpleasant flashbacks to her upsetting dream of so many weeks before.

She stood up, brushed at the pine needles that stuck to her clothing, realizing she had somehow lost her windbreaker. She tried looking for her backpack but remembered she had dropped it when she panicked and ran off.

Alex berated herself for having lost her precious water and food. She hadn't brought much with her up the mountainside, but anything, no matter how small, would taste wonderful. She morosely accepted the fact that she had nothing to eat and began looking around for the best direction to begin her search for the trail. As she walked, she spotted some small, brown and white mushrooms growing on the forest floor and reached down to pick them. Then she remembered she didn't know the difference between edible and poisonous varieties so she sulkily moved on.

Alex reached a clearing that promised an escape route. She released a gasp of relief in spite of increasing hunger pangs in her stomach and legs that were heavy with fatigue. Suddenly her eyes flashed with recognition as she spotted the trail she was seeking just ahead. She began to run, but remembered her lack of energy so slowed her pace. As her feet plodded heavily down the dirt path, they created a cadence that lulled her into a rather mindless state. She moved and panted like an animal, and was surprised that she didn't care. She just wanted to be safe. As she saw the cabins below growing larger, she was filled with new strength and changed her step to a trot and then to a run, swinging her arms freely to enable her to make longer strides.

As she fell onto the little cabin's front porch and tried the door, she realized it was locked. *"Damn!"* The key was back up on the mountain in her lost daypack. *Damn!"* she said again as she pounded the door with her fist. She whirled around and marched toward the motel office, her patience depleted.

CHAPTER 9

"We were so worried about you when you didn't return last night. As it got dark, we called Sheriff Ogden. He said not to worry, that he'd look for you this morning if you weren't back," said the old woman. Her husband leaned protectively toward Alex.

"I'll just call Henry - Sheriff Ogden - and tell him you're okay," said the old man, reaching for the phone.

Alex felt a rising embarrassment and irritation as she realized she was expected to provide some sort of plausible explanation for her disappearance. She couldn't really explain it to herself, so she mumbled her alibi.

"I should have known better than to have hiked so far. I just miscalculated the time. I promise I'll be more careful from now on."

She meekly thanked the couple for their concern and returned to her cabin with the spare key they had given her. Unlocking the door, she stepped inside, tossed the key ring onto the bureau and fell heavily onto the creaking bed. She longed for sleep to take her into dreamless forgetfulness. Every muscle ached and burned, the bump on her head throbbed, and the scratches on her arms and face stung. She closed her eyes and, much to her dismay and irritation, she was suddenly taken back into the nightmare of so many weeks ago once again.

The way my body feels at this point, I might as well *have been torn apart.*

Just as a heavy drowsiness crept over her, pulling her into oblivion, she imagined herself stepping into a dark bubbling pool of hot, steaming water. The image lulled her into a deep sleep.

As she dreamed, she knew she shared the pool with bears and felt strangely comforted.

CHAPTER 10

Over the next two days, Alex took full advantage of the opportunity to rest. She found a small lending library within walking distance and checked out a few old novels she had always been meaning to read but had never found the time.

She discovered a set of comfortable, old rattan chairs on the back porch of her cabin and to her surprise, relished the absence of responsibility while she sat reading. She listened to the nearby stream gurgling and rushing over the rocks. She took short naps in her favorite of the two chairs, and ate snacks of fruit and crackers purchased at the nearby general store. She dragged the quilt outside and cuddled in its soft, reassuring warmth. To Alex, life seemed to be improving.

On her third day of repose, she tired of reading so she wandered down to the little stream. She sat on a large granite rock that jutted out into the water. Multicolored leaves had fallen into the stream and merged magnetically, obstructing the flow around the edge of the rock.

Alex's attention was drawn to the blockage and she rested her chin on her knees, which were drawn up and wrapped with her arms. As more floating debris was caught by the leaf jam, she began to feel a rising irritation. She looked around and found a long stick, which she poked into the mess of leaves, liberating it and watching it float freely down the stream until it disappeared around a bend in the watercourse.

She wondered why she had felt driven to release the leaf jam. She suspected it had something to do with how she had been feeling over the past few months.

But that doesn't make sense. Why should I feel a need to be set free when my life is going so well and my work is so ... compelling.

As she heard the word *compelling* in her mind, Alex felt an uncomfortable sensation as she connected "compelling" with "compulsion."

She felt uneasy at what she had to admit was an ever-growing need for release in her life. But release from what? Wasn't she happy with her work in the advertising firm? Wasn't she advancing in her chosen field and creating quite a reputation at the agency as a real go-getter? Didn't she feel that she was an effective parent? What did all this have to do with compulsion? It didn't make sense to her.

Alex's discomfort increased so she decided to go for a walk to clear her mind. She rambled along the pebble-strewn edge of the stream, kicking stones in her path as she moved along, her fists poked down hard into the pockets of her jeans.

She thought about Rosie and tried to justify the reasons for driving herself so hard in her career as the need to support her child. *I'm providing everything she needs. I can be proud of myself for that. And I want her to be proud of me too!*

But she had to admit how she had accomplished many things in her life without feeling totally complete. There was always an aftermath of emptiness. She had always wondered how much more it would take until she was truly satisfied.

She had always known deep inside that she had collected her college degrees as a way of evoking approval from her parents. And yet it hadn't worked. They never gave her the glowing appreciation she longed for. In fact, at the graduation ceremony where she was to receive her Master's degree in business, her mother had a fainting spell and her father had to help the woman from the hall. As a result, her parents never saw her receive her diploma. She felt the still-smoldering anger toward her mother for having deployed an all too typical maneuver for pulling attention away from others and toward herself.

Whacking at the stones on the path with a stick, Alex trudged on. She wished these uncomfortable memories had not arisen. They were intruding on an otherwise relaxing day.

It doesn't matter what happened in the past or what anyone else thinks of me...or if they approve or not of anything I do. I don't need anything from anybody. I'm doing just fine!

Somehow her discomfort didn't abate. Strange stirrings within her merely contributed to her malaise. She continued walking and considered packing up and going home but she suspected what she was feeling would not be assuaged by a different location. She felt defeated but about what she could not identify. She supposed the strange feeling in the pit of her stomach was hunger so she made her way back to her cabin.

CHAPTER 11

When she arrived at her little cabin, the tilt-back chair on the back porch looked inviting, so she sat down, crunched into an apple and pulled the quilt onto her lap. As she patted it in place, hoping to be able to take a nap and forget her upsetting thoughts, Alex was startled.

The quilt looked strangely different. She held it up in front of her to get a better look. She squinted, trying to identify the difference. There was nothing obvious, but she uneasily suspected that the colors had become brighter, more intense.

She reasoned that it was probably laundry day and her hostess had taken it to wash. But she knew this wasn't right because the quilt was in exactly the same position she had left it before her walk.

She began to feel a rising uneasiness and looked around her. She had the distinct feeling she was not alone. She got up and peered around the sides of the cabin, but aside from a bushy-tailed squirrel who quickly scampered away, there was no one. She entered the cabin, checking the bathroom and the small closet. Nothing.

This is ridiculous. I'm not going to buy into this. I'm going to take a nap as planned...with the quilt!

Alex stomped back out to the porch, sat down, snatched the covering and laid it over her. She closed her eyes, blanked her mind, and allowed sleepiness to overcome her.

But restlessness won out and she opened her eyes. Alex was startled to see a strange woman sitting in the other chair. The woman was studying her with a steady gaze.

Though unnerved, Alex smiled faintly and said, "You startled me. Can I help you with something?"

The woman pointed to the quilt.

"Oh, the quilt. Yes. Oh, it's yours!" Alex said, suddenly understanding and hoping the woman would provide an answer to the mystery of the change in the covering's color. She began to pull the quilt off her legs and hand it to the woman. But the woman shook her head and waved the quilt away impatiently.

Confused, Alex stared at the woman, whose long, wavy hair and dark eyes seemed vaguely familiar. She couldn't determine the woman's age and that alarmed her for some reason. She felt that she was in some sort of strange time warp, where ordinary things could no longer be relied upon.

The woman continued to stare back at Alex and they seemed at an impasse until the woman stood up. She moved as the stream had moved, flowing and swift, but her movement was soundless. She lifted the quilt from Alex's lap and stepped off the porch. She walked to a clear patch of ground a few feet away and spread out the quilt, smoothing it carefully with her hands, which had a particular gracefulness about them. Though toughened, they looked like the hands of an artist.

Satisfied with her work, the woman looked up toward the porch and motioned for Alex to join her.

Although part of her resisted, Alex found herself climbing down from the porch and walking toward this odd visitor. There was something intriguing about this woman, who gestured for her to sit. She folded her legs under her and sat on the ground, somehow knowing she was not to sit upon the quilt. She sensed she was about to be given some sort of instruction.

As she looked intently into the woman's face, Alex felt as if she knew her. Her mind strained to remember where she had seen her before.

Then, suddenly, she knew this woman was the driver of the car at the cafe.

"I saw you a day or so ago down the road at a cafe. You were driving a car, dropped off a man, and later drove away with him. Did you see me?" Alex blurted out, in an attempt to soften the impact of what was happening.

In response, the woman merely pointed to a section of the quilt, where there seemed to be a depiction of a sort of pathway. On one side of it there were shapes cut from dark-colored cloth. And on the other, the shapes were brightly colored. The woman used her ring-bedecked finger to trace the pathway, looking up frequently to make sure Alex was paying strict attention. Then, she pointed with her long, expressive hands at both sides of the path, indicating that they were related. Then she folded her hands in her lap, peering into Alex's face with an expectant look.

Alex knew the woman was waiting for her to respond in some way, but she was unable to fathom what she should do.

As if reading her thoughts, the woman pointed to her mouth and made hand movements indicating talk.

"I don't know what you want me to talk about," Alex said. "I don't even know who you are."

Laughter burst forth from the woman and she replied, rocking with enjoyment, "Of course you do. You just told me I was the woman who was driving that car."

The woman's reply surprised Alex since she had assumed the woman was mute.

"Well, *weren't* you that woman?" Alex asked, feeling as though she had missed the point of a very obvious joke.

"If you say so. Certainly. I was that woman."

Feeling only slightly reassured, Alex recalled the younger woman she had seen in the rear of the car. "And who was that in the back seat?"

"Back seat? No one was in the back seat," the woman stated, frowning and tilting her head, looking perplexed. "It was only myself and the man you saw." The woman smiled an enigmatic smile.

"But I saw a woman in the back seat...a young woman," Alex said, her frustration mounting. She felt ill equipped by her lack of an intellectual explanation for this strange situation.

Suddenly, the woman fell over backward, howling with laughter, arms wrapped around her sides. Tears rolled from her eyes as she cackled. The laughter finally subsided and the woman lay still on the earth, as if in death. Seconds, then minutes passed and there was no movement.

"My God, she's had a heart attack!"

CHAPTER 12

Alex instinctively leapt up and bounded across the quilt to the prostrate woman. As she leaned down to feel for a pulse in the woman's neck, the woman's right eye flashed open, startling her.

"That was very good," said the woman, pulling herself up again to a sitting position and casually picking dry weeds from her skirt. "But try it again to see if you can stay on the path. You stepped right onto a cactus." She pointed to a green patch on the quilt, which was roughly shaped like the saguaro variety of cacti. "But you do that a lot anyway, don't you?"

"I don't know what you're talking about. I was only trying to help you. I thought you had died!" Alex said angrily. She stood up to her full height and crossed her arms solidly over her chest.

"I did. But you weren't supposed to save me. You were supposed to stay on the pathway."

"The pathway? What pathway? I really don't think you and I are on the same wavelength. You see, just a moment ago, you fell backward and looked as if you'd had a heart attack. So I ran over to you to see if I could help. You did lose consciousness, so I guess that's why you don't know what I did." Alex shifted her position and softened her stance, believing she now understood.

"*Who* lost consciousness?" the woman asked. Her eyes pierced Alex's, as her neck craned forward.

"*You* did when you fainted."

"*I* did?" The woman seemed to be intensely interested in Alex's rationale. "Tell me more about this losing consciousness business."

Suspecting she was the butt of some obscure joke, Alex nevertheless attempted once again to explain what had happened. She squatted down on her haunches, hands folded in front of her. She wanted to appear open but ready to run if need be.

"I guess maybe I acted prematurely. I don't have any medical training. It just looked to me like something had happened to you. But I really don't know what else I could have done. I acted on instinct."

"That wasn't instinct," the woman said.

"Then what was it?" Alex's shoulders tightened.

"Stupidity."

"Was it stupidity to try to save your life?" Alex felt the heat of anger rising from her chest into her neck and face.

"It's not *my* life you need to save."

Alex just stared, dumbfounded, into the woman's face.

CHAPTER 13

"Then whose life was it?" Alex's fists knotted and she felt the anger rising higher.

The woman's attitude shifted dramatically from one of challenge to one of sincere concern. She moved close and gently uncurled Alex's fists until her palms and fingers were open and receptive. The movement caused Alex to sit down again.

"Look into your hands," she prompted.

Alex jumped when she saw the rainbow fire arising from the center of her hands. The woman made a calming motion with her lovely hands over the flames. The rainbow of color became a dark, swirling pool.

"Keep watching. Pay close attention," the woman urged.

A face began to appear from deep within the pool.

"Whose face is this?" asked the woman.

"I...I think it's... mine."

"Yes. It's the face of the life you need to save."

Alex's head snapped up, eyes narrowing as she regarded the woman suspiciously.

Their mutually dark eyes locked for what seemed to be endless minutes. In that timeless place, she felt a strange accuracy in what the woman had just revealed to her. She began to feel the vaguely familiar need for freedom, but this time, it felt different. It felt as if it were already a reality.

Suddenly, Alex began to panic. She was terrified but didn't know why. She only knew she felt that her world might come to an end at any moment. Before she could react, she felt herself being pulled away from the ground and experienced floating into nothingness.

She frantically grabbed at the air in a futile attempt to stabilize herself but this only caused her to spin around and around. She became dizzy and ceased her grasping. The spinning stopped. She soon discovered that each time she attempted to grope at anything familiar, the spinning began again. She knew had no choice but to float for what seemed to be an eternity.

In the midst of the nothingness, Alex heard a voice calling her name. Reflexively, she turned her head toward the sound and felt her body touch back down to the ground. But this was altogether a different place.

She found herself in a garden of the most extraordinary plants. They were rainbow-hued and she could not differentiate between foliage and flowers. She heard the sound of gently flowing water, and suspected there might be a waterfall nearby.

Out of the dense growth came two figures. One was the woman. The other was the longhaired man who had appeared with the bear in what Alex had believed had been a dream. They were each dressed in rainbow-patterned clothing, with unusual headdresses of feathers and metallic ribbons that danced lightly in the breeze. Alex looked downward and saw that she was dressed in the same rainbow-colored costume. She was surprised that she wasn't afraid. Instead, she felt strangely calm and almost excited.

She wanted to ask where she was, but when she looked at the two beings standing before her, the words would not come. To gaze into the eyes of others whom she barely knew would ordinarily have been a disquieting experience, but this time she felt calm, at ease and uncharacteristically secure.

The man and woman moved forward to embrace her and her tears began to flow. They held her as she sobbed.

After a long while, Alex's crying stopped and she looked into the dark eyes of these two strange people.

A smile radiated from the depth of her being as she began to feel as if she had come home.

CHAPTER 14

"I don't understand what I'm feeling," Alex mused. "But I don't seem to be really concerned about the reasons."

They all burst into laughter and Alex realized she hadn't laughed in that way since she was a little girl. She didn't even know what was so funny but enjoyed the deep feeling of well-being.

The woman motioned to Alex and the man to sit with her on the multi-colored grass. The woman was the first to speak.

"You have passed over the first threshold."

"What does that mean?"

"Be careful. You could throw yourself backward and then you'd have to do it all over again!" The man winked conspiratorially at the woman and they laughed again. Alex frowned as the joke eluded her.

"Do *what* all over again?" Alex's whined. She felt a rising fear as the spinning began again. She shook her head to clear it and felt herself beginning to float upward. As her terror grew, she pleaded for help.

Instantly, she returned lightly to her spot on the grass and the woman calmed her by passing her hand downward in front of Alex's face and all the way down to her knees.

"You've just passed the second threshold," the man said, smiling kindly.

Alex looked at him blankly. "By doing what?"

He merely smiled.

Then it dawned on her. "You mean by asking you to help me?"

He smiled again.

"What's so important about that?"

"Why haven't you asked for help before now?" he asked.

"Well, obviously. I never needed it before. I've always taken care of things myself," she said, tossing her hair from her shoulder nervously.

"Why would you do that?" asked the woman.

Alex looked at them and wondered if they were dull-witted. She frowned at them as she answered.

"Because I'm an adult. And adults have responsibilities. And besides, not that I'm bragging or anything, but I can generally do things quicker and...well, better, than most people," she said.

The man and woman just looked at each other as if seriously concerned by her answer.

"What?" she asked, feeling slightly dizzy again.

"So you think you're an adult, eh?" asked the man, piercing into her face with his dark eyes.

"Of course I'm an adult," Alex said, "I have responsibilities."

"You said that before," said the woman.

"Well, I do!"

"Uh-huh," said the woman, brushing dust from her dress.

"Oh," said Alex, suddenly feeling an understanding. "I get it. You two are part of one of those New Agey cults

I've heard about. Where you just meditate all day and don't believe in responsibility."

She rose quickly as if to leave. "Well, I'm not buying it. I believe firmly in responsibility and I'm not giving it up for you or for anyone!"

"So do we," said the man, gently.

Totally confused, Alex hesitated. She was unnerved by a reluctance to leave these people, at the same time she suspected the worst of them.

"What *is* responsibility?" he asked, leaning forward and looking deeply into her eyes. "But before you answer, why don't you just sit down. It's very hard to see you way up there." He winked at the woman and she grinned back.

As if pulled down to the grass by an outside force, Alex sat with a thump. She knew they were waiting for her answer.

"It's, well, it's...," she said, stammering and distressed that she felt so unsure. "It's being an adult."

Then she saw the looks on their faces and realized she needed to take a different tack.

"Okay, it's doing what you have to do."

"Hmm," said the man, digesting her words. "Doing what you *have* to do. Um-hmm. I see."

"Oh, I see. Okay. Doing what I *want* to do. Is that better?" Alex felt triumphant.

"Not much," the woman said, still brushing at the dust and appearing to be bored by Alex's responses.

"And *are* you doing what you want to do?" asked the man.

"Well, of course I am. I have responsib..."

"Oh, here we go again," said the woman, rolling her eyes and lying down on the grass. She closed her eyes as if to end the conversation.

Alex looked to the man but his face was blank and he remained silent. She felt an all too familiar feeling arising in her chest. It felt like a cold knife in her heart. In the past it had always accompanied the pain of rejection and the anguish of worthlessness. Her eyes began to well up so she looked away to prevent the two from seeing the tears.

"What are you crying for, Alex?" asked the woman, who was now sitting at her side. Her voice had become soft and Alex ventured out of her pain. She saw caring in the woman's eyes but this only made her cry harder.

The tears finally abated and the woman asked again, "What are you crying for, Alex?"

"I'm crying for myself," said Alex, surprised at her response.

"Go on," the woman prompted, putting a hand lightly on Alex's back.

"I'm crying because I really don't know what I want. And because I don't think I'm happy. I think I'm worn out," she said, her throat catching and tears flowing again.

"Alex, are you being responsible right now?" asked the man.

Startled, Alex didn't know what to say.

"What does that word, 'responsible,' mean anyway?" asked the man.

"I don't know," she said wearily. "Maybe something to do with the ability to respond?" She looked at him questioningly.

"Yes, and what have you just been doing?"

"Responding?" she said, encouraged but not yet totally sure of where he was taking her.

"To whom?"

"To you, of course."

Then, something from within her lit up. "Oh," she said, hesitating but feeling the impact of each word. "To *myself*!"

Alex felt a release of tension in her chest. The icy knife was gone and in its place a warm vibration. It felt like relief. It may even have felt like love.

CHAPTER 15

Alex opened her eyes and saw the red-blue sky of sunset. She stretched luxuriously like a cat and felt the quilt underneath her. She sat up slowly, relishing delight in the moment.

She vaguely expected to see the dark-haired woman, but concluded that she had only been dreaming again. As she rose to her feet, however, she saw a note pinned to the quilt.

"Join us later. We'll be by to pick you up around 8," the note said. It was signed, "Betty and Mack."

Truly surprised at her willingness now to accept her experience as more than a dream, she chuckled to herself.

Hmm. Well, they actually have human names! She stuffed the note into her jeans pocket and went inside to shower.

As the steamy water washed over her face, Alex reveled in the feeling. She laughed aloud at the pleasure of it.

I feel so clean! She marveled as she heard the thought pass through her mind, but shrugged it off as she reached for the bottle of shampoo. As she scrubbed her scalp and made billows of lather, she sculpted her hair into a wild style that made her laugh aloud.

Later, hair dryer in hand, Alex mused at this unexpected turn of events. *They seem harmless enough.* She smiled at the thought of her two new friends, Betty and Mack, strange as they were.

As she dressed, she felt excited at the prospect of what they might have planned for the evening.

Some minutes after eight o'clock, Alex heard a car drive up. She peered out the window and recognized the rusty car from the cafe. She found herself grinning.

What the heck! Why not? she thought as she grabbed her jacket and ran out to meet Betty and Mack.

"Where are we headed?" she asked as she settled herself in the back seat. Betty was driving and Mack turned himself in the passenger seat so he could converse with Alex.

"You'll see," Mack said.

Alex felt a bit unnerved by the vague answer, but decided to just sit back and enjoy the ride.

Some time later, Betty stopped the car. The darkness of the night obscured any clear view of the terrain, but as she stepped out of the car, Alex felt sand under her feet and guessed they were in a desert.

Mack told her to follow him and Betty brought up the rear behind Alex. They walked for what seemed to be at least a mile, then they began a slow, gradual climb through a stand of large, red sandstone boulders.

Finally, Mack motioned for Alex to sit on one of the large rocks that had a flat surface. The man and woman sat on either side of her.

The view was spectacular. The silvery moon illumined the desert below in a mysterious blue-gray light. It was lovely.

They sat in silence for a while, then Mack asked, "So have you been thinking about responsibility?"

Pulled from her reverie, Alex whipped her head around to face him.

"What?" she asked, not sure she had heard his question.

"Responsibility. You know. Being able to respond to yourself."

Once again, dizziness overtook her. Alex feared she would fall off the rock and plummet down the mountain, so she desperately groped for something to hang onto. The dizziness merely increased.

She heard her voice, as if from a distance, calling, "Why don't you help me?"

"We *are* helping you," a voice responded. "Just stop grasping. You'll slow down."

She stopped her frantic scrambling and let go. She landed softly back on the rock.

Betty leaned over and looked deeply into Alex's eyes. "Don't you get it yet? The dizziness is caused by your fearful need to control everything." She patted Alex's arm.

Alex stared at her, not sure of what the woman meant. But she knew now that the spinning always stopped when she stopped trying to hold onto something familiar. Maybe this is what Betty meant.

They sat in silence until Mack broke the stillness.

"I once knew a man who was a crane operator. You know, in the construction industry."

Alex nodded.

"He was very good at his job but he wasn't that great with his coworkers. They used to say he wasn't a good listener...just never wanted to hear anyone else's ideas...always insisted on 'going by the book.'"

Mack took a long drink of the water in his dented metal canteen, then wiped his mouth with the back of his hand.

"Well, one day, he was lifting about two tons of iron to move to another spot. As usual, he was doing it exactly the way he had been doing it for years."

Alex was surprised at her enthusiasm for Mack's story. Ordinarily, hearing about a crane operator wouldn't have held any interest for her whatsoever. She leaned back against the rock and listened carefully.

"This guy was so determined to move this iron in the way he always had...and he prided himself in doing things that way...that he ignored his coworkers' shouts to stop his engine. He merely waved them off, irritated at their interruption."

Alex's eyes widened at what she sensed would be a dramatic climax to the story.

"What this guy refused to see because of his insistence in controlling the situation his way, was a small dog who had run into the pile of iron rails. The other men were trying to tell him to stop before the dog was crushed."

Alex waited for the inevitable conclusion. But Mack remained silent. Alex heard nothing except a distant lonely cry of a night bird. She began to perspire, although the evening air was cool.

The dreaded dizziness loomed within her. "Oh, no, not again!" she cried.

Alex started to reach out for Betty's arm, but suddenly realized that all she had to do was calm herself. The dizziness ceased immediately.

She looked at Mack for several moments.

"So what you're trying to tell me is that I'm like the little dog?" she asked. "Just running around putting myself in dangerous situations? Like this one." Her attempt at humor failed.

"Try again," said Mack, adjusting his position on the rock.

"What? You're saying I'm like the crane operator?" she asked, totally confused.

"Are you?" he asked, his face a model of innocence.

"I wouldn't let that happen!" Alex insisted. "I wouldn't want that dog to be hurt."

"But it got hurt anyway," said Betty.

Alex blinked her eyes and shook her head slightly to clear her mind.

"So you're implying that even though I wouldn't want the dog to get hurt, I'd hurt it anyway?"

"Look at the crane operator," said Mack. "How does he play into your life?"

"There's no connection at all," said Alex. "I'm not like him. He doesn't care about the people he works with and he just wants to control every...." She froze as she heard what she said.

"Congratulations!" said Betty, reaching over and pounding Alex's back hard several times.

Alex didn't know whether to feel happy or merely irritated at the acknowledgment. But before she could decide how she felt, Mack continued.

"Somewhere along your path of life, you created the idea that you should do everything yourself. You learned to do things well but also to control everything in your life so you could depend upon your way of doing things. You thought this was taking responsibility.

"But it was a withdrawal from life, from your pain. You insist upon doing everything yourself because you are afraid to let new ideas or people into your circle of defenses."

Feeling herself caught in her own game, Alex surrendered and admitted, "My defenses?"

"Of course, your defenses. What do you think we've been trying to help you knock down?" asked the woman, feigning irritation.

"But why? Without them, the world would overwhelm me. People would take advantage. I wouldn't have any life of my own," she said.

"*With* them you have no life of your own. In fact, no life at all. You have been living a lie," said the long-haired man.

She looked at him incredulously. She feared that her rising confusion and anger might throw her again into the dizzy spinning.

"He means that you haven't been living your true life. You've been living a life that you believed you *should* live. Why do you think you've been crying inside for freedom?"

Alex's head jerked and her eyes widened at Betty's accuracy.

"The freedom you want is the freedom to be yourself, to be authentic. Without it, you will die a miserable death, internally and externally. You will have contributed nothing to yourself, to your daughter, or to the world."

"D...die?"

"Yes, that's what was beginning to happen to you. Didn't you see that you were like *both* the crane operator *and* the little dog in Mack's story?"

"Well...maybe. But I didn't think it was because I was literally dying."

"Well, it was. And now we will teach you how to die properly," said Betty.

"What?" Alex leapt up and lost her balance. As she tried to keep herself from falling off the rock, she looked quickly around for an escape route. She scrambled over the rock onto the trail.

"You people are insane!" she called over her shoulder as she ran, "This little therapy session of yours is over!"

CHAPTER 16

"Where are you going?" Betty called. She was smoothing her skirt, looking bemused and almost unconcerned.

"Where do you think I'm going? I'm not about to let you kill me! I knew you were up to something and now I know what!" Alex stumbled and fell hard onto her knees.

"Come back and sit down, you're just going to make yourself dizzy again," said Betty. She patted the rock beside her, indicating the place to sit.

"Right now I'm not worried about getting dizzy. I'm trying to save my life!" Alex snapped, reeling in circles now and losing her bearings. She had torn a hole in one knee of her jeans and she felt blood oozing from a deep cut.

"That's exactly what we're trying to help you do, too."

Alex stopped her frantic thrashing and looked first at Betty, then at Mack. Her instinct said that things were not as they seemed and she was actually safe. Hesitatingly, she cautiously moved back to the rock, where she sat down with a thump and peered warily first at Betty, then at Mack.

"To find your freedom, you must die to old ways. You must cut into the ways in which you perceive things and dissect them until you find their heart," Betty said.

"And when you find their heart, you will find your own," Mack added.

"Let me tell you a story," said the woman, smiling.

"Oh, no, not another story!" moaned Alex.

Betty laughed and pulled on Alex's jacket to indicate that she wanted her to sit closer.

"It begins a long, long time ago in the days when the Great Mother reigned over the land and the lives of the people. The times were good and everyone had a voice in how their communities were to be run. The Great Mother took care of her people and healed their illnesses, their sorrows, and helped them grow productive crops.

"But then, one day, strange peoples began to descend on the villages. They had forsaken the teachings of the Great Mother and began to worship the god of war. They swarmed down into the villages and communities and burned all of the homes, raped the women and killed everyone. In one village, the warrior leader determined that it would be to his great advantage to kill the High Priestess of the community. He sought her out and drove a spear through her heart. He left her to die in a field that had been burned by his soldiers. He gathered his troops and they left to find yet another community to pillage. The Priestess's blood ran red into the earth and she lay there for three days.

"At the end of those three days, wolves came down from the hills and tore her body apart. Some of the wolves carried parts of her to the north, the place of wisdom; other wolves carried parts of her to the east, the place of illumination; more wolves carried parts of her to the south, the place of love and compassion; and other wolves carried parts of her to the west, the place of the dreamer.

"Time went by and the Great Mother grew sad and angry at what had happened to her land and people. So she walked on the land and lay down. She dreamed of what had happened to the Priestess, so she awoke and called all of the Priestess's parts to her. She placed the Priestess's head from the north on her own shoulders, the parts from the east on her forehead, the parts from the south on her heart, and the parts from the west on her belly. She prayed that the Priestess would come back to life and once again share the love and wholeness that had been such a natural part of daily life before the warriors had come.

"The Priestess awoke and saw that she was alive. She looked at her body and was pleased. She thanked the Great Mother within her for giving her life. But then she saw that the spear was still in her heart.

"'Great Mother,' she cried in despair, 'you have made me live again, but this spear that killed me is still in my heart.'

"'Yes,' said the Great Mother, 'and it will remain so in order to keep your heart open and remind you that love is the most important thing in the world.'

"And so the Priestess traveled throughout the land and healed the people's sicknesses of mind and body. They would come to her and say:

"'Priestess, my husband has run away with another woman, my heart is breaking!', or 'Priestess, my daughter is very ill and may die, it hurts so bad in my heart.', or 'Priestess, I have no money, my crops have failed, it feels like a knife in my heart.'

"She would turn to them and say, 'Yes, there is a knife in your hearts. It is there to remind you to love.'"

Alex was transfixed as Betty concluded the story but was aware of a rising discomfort in the pit of her stomach. She broke the silence.

"I don't understand how the story has anything to do with me. Do I have to die and go around with a knife in my heart? That sounds pretty morbid." Alex heard herself whining again.

"You already have a knife in your heart," replied Betty, looking directly into Alex's eyes. "What you have to die to is your need to deny it. We all have pain. We all suffer. But the suffering is always made worse if we run away from difficult parts of our lives."

Alex felt a cloudiness descending over her mind. "Do you mean I ran away by coming up here?"

Mack laughed. "No, by coming up here, you were actually running *to* your life."

"Now I'm totally confused," admitted Alex. She looked at Betty. "Does this have anything to do with the time you fell over on the quilt and I tried to save your life?"

"I'll ask you again: *Whose* life?"

"Okay, okay. *My* life," said Alex with a little smile curving on her lips. "But I still don't get what I'm supposedly running away from."

Betty and Mack just looked at her. Moments passed and Alex squirmed in increasing discomfort.

"Alright," she said. "You two keep implying that how I'm living my life is what I'm running away from. Is that right?" She looked at them expectantly, hoping for a definitive response.

"It's not what you're *doing*, Alex," said Mack, smoothing his long hair. "It's what's *underneath* it all."

"Underneath? I'm not following you," Alex said, frustrated once again.

CHAPTER 17

"Follow the quilt," Betty said.

"Follow the...quilt?" Alex asked.

"You noticed the quilt changed hue?" asked Mack.

"Yes."

"The quilt is like life. It changes as you change. The colors intensified because you expanded your perception."

"How did I do that?"

"Your former self was killed by the beast in your dream and then you met your new self in the woods on the mountain," said the long-haired man.

Alex gasped. "How did you know about that dream?"

"Your brother was the beast who killed you," he replied calmly, ignoring her question.

Her eyes were riveted on his. Alex feared for her sanity and her life.

"Do you remember what I told you on the mountain?" he continued.

"But I thought that was a dream," she replied hesitantly, not trusting where he might be leading her.

"It was only a dream then because you weren't ready to hear what I told you," Mack said.

Alex now recalled how, in what she thought was a dream, she was able to change the colors of the rainbows in her hands by merely changing her thoughts. Then she remembered what the man had looked like: he looked like Mack. She shook her head in disbelief.

"Remember I told you that the colors in your hands indicated a work you'd be doing?" Mack asked. "Well, you've already begun that work by learning that you create your perceptions and your reality, that they don't create you."

"So what you're saying is that my life is a result of how I perceive it?" Alex strained her mind for understanding.

"Exactly." Betty pounded her back again. Alex flinched and wasn't sure she liked all the back pounding.

"But life just is what it is. People just have to adjust and make the best of it. I can't change that," she said.

"From your limited perspective, you're right. Life is something that's done to you. Right?"

Suspecting another trap, Alex resisted answering. But the words had hit home. They troubled her but ignited a feeling of hope that she would soon understand. She sat, wondering about this strange world of new ideas and experiences. Betty and Mack sat by her in silence.

After a while, Alex stood and stretched, looking out over the terrain, and feeling strangely larger than usual. She also felt a kind of strength or courage that was new to her. She looked around for Betty and saw her standing at a distance, looking back at her.

She started to speak, but the woman made a signal with her hand for silence. She pointed to the distant mountains.

"Tomorrow you will go back up to the mountains to find your brother."

Alex's voice shook as she spoke. "Go back up there? I'd be crazy to do that!"

The woman cut her off. "There is no craziness here. It is only found in the life you have been living. Now you must make a decision. Do you want to live or do you want to die?" The woman stood straight and commanding.

"Of course I want to live. But I almost lost my life up there. I don't want to do that again."

"Then don't go up there with the same stupidities. Don't you remember anything we've been teaching you?"

"I'm not sure," Alex hesitated, her voice softening. "All this has happened so fast. It's been so bizarre. I don't know what to think anymore."

Alex approached Betty and asked, "Will you teach me how to do what you are asking me to do?"

The woman smiled and put out her hands. "I am so happy you have decided." She took Alex's hands and hugged her. "You may not be so stupid after all."

They both laughed and linked arms with Mack as they all walked down the mountainside to map out the task for the next day.

CHAPTER 18

Alex floated above a lifeless body on the ground. It looked strangely familiar. She recognized it as her own. "But how could I be up here and down there at the same time?"

"Follow the Quilt," came a voice.

She looked down again and saw that the terrain was like a quilt, with distinct patterns and lines to follow, as if they were pathways. She saw that the body below was situated in a particularly dark area. She became aware of the hairy, lumbering form of a creature moving away from the body. It was moving along one of the lines. From her perspective, she could see ahead of the creature and where it was going. It was moving directly toward a small figure playing in a grassy area.

"My God, that's my daughter!"

"Your ordinary reaction is to panic and to see only one option. Choose something different. Her life depends upon it," the voice counseled.

"What can I choose? I have no options!"

"Then your daughter is already dead," the voice said.

"Help me! I don't know what you mean!"

Silence. The voice did not respond. Alex could only think of how she could save her daughter. Suddenly, she remembered her hands. Logic told her this was nonsense, but she dismissed the thought and thrust her hands toward the creature. The movement carried her down to the ground and directly in the hairy beast's path. It looked at her, startled, and then snarled, moving toward her. She pushed her hands toward its face, but the creature kept coming. She looked squarely into the eyes of the beast, its jaws snapping viciously. She held her gaze, somehow knowing she must hold her position no matter what.

The beast stopped its movement and growled menacingly.

"Look at the little girl," it said roughly, motioning toward her daughter with its hairy paw.

Alex looked over her shoulder and saw a fruit tree where the girl had been.

"Where is she?" she demanded, panicking.

The creature laughed a gritty laugh. "She was never there. I used her image in your mind to get you here."

"Why? So you could kill me again?" Alex asked cuttingly.

"I already did. That was to get your attention too! I've been trying to do that all of your life," the beast said, responding with what looked like a grin. "Finally, it worked!"

CHAPTER 19

Alex awoke feeling groggy. As she slid her hands up over the covers, she felt the soft textures of the quilt. She opened her eyes to find herself back in her little cabin. As she sat up, she suspected she'd had another troubling dream and her sense of time was jumbled, so she was puzzled at her lighthearted state of mind. Sun was streaming through the windows and the late morning sounds of birds and an occasional car passing by added to her mood.

She hopped out of bed, quickly pulled on her jeans and a soft sweatshirt and went outside. She stood on her porch, stretching languidly, and looked out over the honey-colored mountains. She recognized a deep feeling of peace that had been growing in her over the last few days. Something was shifting within her. There were feelings of newness along with frequent spasms of joy in her gut. As she looked at the terrain around her cabin, she wondered what was happening to her. She considered that even if it had all been a dream or an hallucination, something about it had changed her.

Well, whatever it is, I like it. She bent down to touch a scrubby plant growing by her porch steps.

She stepped lightly off the porch and began walking toward the path to the mountains. Her eyes caught a glimpse of something in the early morning shadows. It was about halfway up the trail and she wondered what it was and why she had missed it on her first walk. She squinted and tried to force her eyes to focus on what the dark shape was. It was roundish and seemed to be a hole in the side of the mountain. She wished she had a pair of binoculars. She decided to ask the innkeepers if they had a pair she could borrow.

As she strolled over to the main lodge, she thought about the quilt and about Betty, who seemed inexorably connected to it in some way. She recalled some information she'd heard once about shamans who dealt in realities beyond ordinary comprehension. She wondered if Betty was one of these people. But for the life of her she couldn't imagine why a shaman might take any interest in her rather mundane, rather un-spiritual life. Alex had always held a strong belief that if she worked hard, did what was expected of her, and didn't veer off the road well-traveled, she would live a satisfactory life. She had never considered that there were any alternatives to that belief. Now questions were arising. This isolated environment gave her more clarity of mind than did the city. Perhaps not *more* clarity, but at least a different kind. Discovering herself thinking about possible changes to her life and lifestyle, she shook her head and stopped walking.

What the hell am I doing? This is crazy! I've worked too hard to get where I am to let some bizarre and totally unreal experiences pull me off track!

She turned around and headed for her cabin with the intention of packing and going home.

CHAPTER 20

Reaching for the door, Alex spied a note pinned to it. She pulled it free and unfolded it.

"Meet us at the cave at sunset."

Her faced blanched, she began shaking, and she realized that what she had seen on the side of the mountain was the entrance to a cave. She felt disturbed that, once again, these strange people were calling her to meet them for what she was sure would be another unpleasant undertaking.

"No! Not this time. They're going to be really disappointed because I'm not meeting them in a cave or anywhere! I'm leaving!"

Alex crumpled the note, threw it on the ground, and ripped open the screen door. She stomped inside, intending to throw her clothes into her suitcase and leave immediately.

Betty was sitting on the bed.

"What are you doing here?" Alex asked angrily.

"Just thought I'd help you with your packing," the woman said, smiling sweetly. She was smoothing the quilt nonchalantly as she spoke.

Caught off guard, Alex spun around toward the door as an escape. She slammed into Mack's muscular form as he came through the doorway.

Feeling trapped and in danger, Alex looked around for an alternative route. Finding none, her mind raced.

"Yes, I was going to leave. I have to get back to my daughter," she said, trying to remain calm.

"The only problem with that is that you're not ready to go back to your daughter," Betty said, still smiling innocently.

"What is *that* supposed to mean," said Alex, frightened but determined not to show it.

"It means you haven't finished your quest," said Mack, settling himself comfortably on a nearby chair.

The door was now unprotected and Alex inched her way toward it.

Betty and Mack began laughing riotously, holding their bellies, their eyes tearing with merriment. Mack was laughing so hard he couldn't speak, so only jabbed his finger repeatedly at the door as if to warn Alex of something.

She ignored his absurd gesturing and reached for the doorknob. As she yanked on it, the door opened with a swoosh and she was catapulted outside. The momentum knocked her from the porch and onto the ground. She pulled herself up to stand, brushing dirt from her jeans. Strangely, she began to reconsider her decision to leave. She stopped brushing and just stood.

This is nuts. Why would I even consider staying here?

"We can't keep you here against your will, Alex. But I have a sense that, deep down, you really want to stay and see this through," said the woman gently. She stood near Alex, with a sincere expression of understanding on her face.

Alex stared at her, then somehow believed the truth in what Betty had said. She could feel something letting go inside and sensed she could go on. It made no logical sense but she knew instinctively that her decision must be made outside of all reason.

"All right, so if you two are going to give me a cave tour, we'd better get started," she said, determined to find courage and get on with this next challenge.

"Yes, Ma'am," replied Mack, giving her an exaggerated salute.

Alex groused to herself as she followed them toward the trailhead. "Oh brother, a couple of shamans named Betty and Mack of all things. With all they're putting me through, they could at least have exotic names like Magic Feather or Merlin or Swami Knows-it-all or..."

CHAPTER 21

By the time they reached the cave's mouth, Alex was panting hard. She stopped, bent over to catch her breath, and tried to communicate her windedness to her companions by waving her hand about.

When she could finally stand again, they were gone. She looked around and, not seeing them, sat down on a rock just inside the entrance to the opening in the mountain. Vaguely, she heard water dripping from within the cave. The sound lulled her and she rather enjoyed her rocky vista. She picked up a small stone and turned it around in her hand, liking its smooth, cool surface.

As she sat rolling the little stone in her hand, listening to the dripping sounds behind her and watching birds zoom up and down the canyon in front of her, Alex thought about her precious daughter, Rosie.

Rosie had been only three when Alex had divorced David. The whole thing had been surprisingly amicable so Alex believed the child was not terribly traumatized by the breakup. David continued to see Rosie often and provided her with everything he could in the absence of their living together as a family. Alex liked David. He was a good man. But she had believed she didn't love him in the way she thought she should in a marriage. So she asked for a divorce, feeling that perhaps he was too good a provider and that she was in danger of losing her independence.

But now she sat wondering if she had made a mistake. She knew David had never intruded on her space and had always encouraged her to do whatever she wanted to do.

But now, she also recalled how Rosie had often said she wished she had a "stay-at-home mommy." She always felt so stretched to the limit when she had to juggle work pressures and commitments with her daughter's needs. She remembered how recently she had completely forgotten an appointment with Rosie's second grade teacher and how shocked and embarrassed she was when the woman spoke to her the next day about it.

As the breeze picked up and blew a strand of her hair in her face, Alex brushed it away. As she held the hair out of her eyes, she reflected upon how she had always believed that her schedule and her stress level would change. She had continued to push herself ahead in her business based upon this belief. But sitting here and now, she felt a wave of doubt and sadness envelop her.

"What have I been doing? When did I allow Rosie to slip off my priority list?" Speaking softly to herself, she heard her voice break and she burst into sobs.

As her crying abated, she swiped at her wet face with her sleeve and punched her hand into a pocket to search for a tissue. Finding none, she wiped her nose with the hem of her sweatshirt.

"Great! Now I'm a soggy mess and all alone on a mountaintop - again!"

"No, not alone." Betty emerged from the cave entrance and sat down nearby on a large rock, startling a grey lizard who scuttled underneath it.

"Where *were* you?" said Alex, accusingly.

"Right in there," Betty said, pointing back into the cave. "We were preparing the cave to welcome you." Smiling, she reached over and pushed more hair out of Alex's face.

Alex was surprised at this show of motherliness, but said nothing.

"Welcome me? What does that mean?"

"It means you are ready to do some traveling," replied the woman.

"Oh-oh, what does that mean?" Alex moaned, suspecting Betty wouldn't be forthcoming with an answer.

Betty continued to smile. She put her arm around Alex's shoulder and gave a little squeeze, then let go.

"I would think you'd welcome this opportunity. Given what you've just realized about your priorities."

Alex stopped, shocked at how the woman always seemed to know what she was thinking.

"Isn't anything I think private at all?"

"Well, that depends," said Betty.

"On what?"

"On what your need for privacy is based on."

Alex's eyes narrowed, and she felt slightly suspicious at the same time, intrigued. "Go on," she said.

"Up until now, you kept things hidden from others because you needed to keep them hidden from yourself."

In her gut, Alex felt the truth of what Betty was telling her. She felt the coolness of the rock underneath her, calming and soothing.

"Do you understand why you didn't want to see these things within you?"

"I think so...but I'm not sure."

"Fear," said Betty, nonchalantly.

"Fear of what?" Alex began to feel dizzy. She took several deep breaths and tried to relax.

"Fear of the things you'd created to cover up the things you were *really* afraid of. That's a lot of fear."

"But," Alex replied, stammering, "aren't they things anyone might be afraid of."

"We're not talking about anyone. We're talking about you," said Betty. She picked up the little stone that slipped out of Alex's hand when she had begun to cry. "You've been holding that beach ball in the tub for too long!"

"What beach ball?" Alex asked.

"Imagine that early in your life someone told you that you would experience dire consequences if you didn't hold a large beach ball under under the surface of the water in a big tub. So like a good girl, you held it down and continued to hold it down all your life."

Betty paused. "Think about how sore and tired your muscles would be!" She shook her head as if seeing the image.

"Then, one day, you realized how silly the whole thing was, and that you could release the ball any time you wanted to and bad things were not going to happen just because you let a beach ball pop up to the surface of a tub of water."

Alex was listening.

"But then, after you released the ball, you fell in a heap beside the tub because all of your energy - your life force - had gone into holding that ball down for so long. Your body, your mind, and your spirit were exhausted."

Alex felt a tug of recognition. Finally, this was beginning to make some sort of sense.

"This is why you were drawn here," said Betty. She handed Alex the smooth little rock. "You have been holding your life force down for too long."

Alex accepted the stone and looked into Betty's dark eyes.

Softly she said, "Yes, I know."

CHAPTER 22

Betty told Alex to wait outside the cave until they were ready for her. Alex stood looking out at the disappearing sun and the colors it made on the terrain.

She thought about how very tired she really was - and had been for some time. She had been shrugging it off and involving herself more deeply in her work than ever. She now considered the possibility that something had been trying to get her attention and she had been ignoring it. Her physical and emotional weariness was a final call. She began to understand that what she had been experiencing here in the mountains was no mistake.

Furrowing her brow, she wondered if Betty and Mack weren't blessings in disguise. She shook her head, struggling with the questions of why they were spending so much time and energy trying to help her.

She wondered to herself why anyone would go to such lengths for a stranger. She examined what might be in it for them. What if they were recruiting her for some sort of cult? Pictures of white slavery, mind control, and never seeing her daughter again played across her mind.

At the same time she feared the worst, a part of her was absolutely calm. Alex didn't know what to do with these conflicting emotions. Should she run or should she stay?

Betty appeared again at her side. "It's up to you, Alex. We will not hold you here against your will. What we are offering must be with your consent."

By now, Alex was getting used to her thoughts being known, so she turned to Betty. "I need to know why you're putting so much into working with me. I need to know what you will get out of it."

Betty hesitated, cleared her throat, then spoke. "Your need to know stands in the way of the true answers you seek. For now, I'll just say that this is the work we do."

"But why me?"

"Because you asked for help," replied Betty.

"Me? I asked for your help? I didn't even know you existed until you showed up. So how could I have asked you anything?"

"You didn't ask for us in particular. And you weren't consciously aware you needed help. But your state of mind and the edge you were fast moving toward sent out a general call for assistance."

"What edge?" Alex asked, wrapping her arms defensively across her chest.

"The one you almost fell over when you were being chased."

The nightmare, thought Alex. "Well, I didn't fall over, did I?"

"But the beast got you, didn't it?" asked Betty.

Alex nodded, feeling queasy in the pit of her stomach.

"Don't you see that you had important work to do before you jumped off the cliff? Can you understand what the beast was doing for you?"

"*For* me?" asked Alex. "*To* me, you mean."

"I meant what I said," said Betty firmly.

By now, Mack had joined them and was listening quietly off to one side in the shadows of the cave's entrance.

Alex realized he was there and looked to him for support. He just smiled.

"He did a good job," Mack said, picking up a stick and peeling its bark.

"Good job?" said Alex. "He tore me apart!"

"That's right," said Betty. "And why do you think that was necessary?"

Alex thought about defending herself again, but a sweet inner stillness overcame her resistance. She closed her open mouth and stood silently in front of Betty and Mack, looking to them for the next move.

Mack looked at Betty and something unspoken passed between them. "What have you lost since you've arrived here?" he asked.

"Lost?" Alex wasn't sure what he meant. "I don't think I lost anything. Oh, you mean the key to my cabin?"

He laughed. "Not to your cabin."

Alex knew they were toying with her. "Okay. I'll play along. If not the cabin key, what key?"

"The one that has been locking you up," Betty replied.

"Uh...does this have something to do with the beach ball?" she asked shrewdly.

Betty and Mack grabbed her in a three-way bear hug, surprising her and knocking her off balance. As she struggled to right herself, they let go and she saw in their eyes a look that seemed to be love. Deep down within her, she hoped it was.

CHAPTER 23

One on either side, Betty and Mack led Alex into the cave. It was cool and damp and the sound of dripping water echoed against the walls. Mack held a small flashlight with a remarkably powerful beam that lit their pathway clearly. Alex could see the rocks and outcroppings along the way, made slick by the moisture in the cave. Some were beautiful limestone pillars and draperies, while others were still in the process of becoming the lovely cave formations. She heard her footsteps reverberating throughout the passages, along with an occasional swoosh which she guessed came from the wings of bats. She was surprised at her lack of fear. Rather, it felt like an adventure. An adventure with two friends.

She smiled to herself at that thought. Strange how these people had woven their way into her life within such a short period of time. It was as if they knew her better than anyone ever had. This was reassuring and a very pleasant awareness. She was amazed that she was willing to admit this, especially since she knew they knew all her secrets.

As they walked, she considered those secrets. What were they? Why did they exist at all? What purpose did they serve? She sensed they were connected in some way to what Betty had said about the beach ball and the beast in her dream. But why were her little secrets so significant to warrant all this?

She reexamined the questions rattling around in her mind. She knew Betty and Mack thought those things she had kept secret - or private - were important. So she looked again at what they were.

She stumbled on a rock and as she regained her footing, she suddenly remembered how she had stopped communicating with David. She paused and recalled her reason at the time as being that she was getting too busy with her work to spend as much time talking with him. But what her gut was telling her now belied that reason. She began to sense the truth. She realized she had stopped talking to him because he had wanted to deepen their relationship. She recalled his telling her that he felt they'd reached the next stage of their partnership, where the typical problems of the first few years of marriage had been resolved and they could now focus on getting to know the other on deeper levels. She knew that meant the dreaded word, "intimacy."

Alex looked up and realized she had she had better hurry if she was to keep up with Betty and Mack. She trudged on, thinking about what David had said. Why would she have been so afraid to do what he suggested? What was it about intimacy that frightened her so?

Concentrating on this question, she rounded a corner and was surprised to see a huge room, filled with the light of several battery-powered lanterns. She conjectured that Mack must have put them there earlier. The room was lovely. Curtains of ages-old formations hung from the ceiling. Stalactites and stalagmites were everywhere, some touching the other to create solid pillars of sparkling beauty.

Alex was beguiled. The visual loveliness was enhanced by the delicate sounds of water flowing somewhere below and the drip, drip, drip from the wall behind her.

"Oh, this is wonderful," she said, turning around and around to gain the full impact of the place.

"We knew you'd like it," said Mack, who was sitting cross-legged on a small blanket he had folded on the earthen floor.

Alex smiled, then feigned suspicion. "I suppose I should ask you now why you've brought me here."

Mack laughed. "You're beginning to know us well."

Alex looked around for Betty and saw that she was turning off the lanterns, one by one. Stomach clenching, Alex asked why she was dimming the light, but Betty didn't answer her.

Finally, when there was only one torch still lit, Betty sat down on another small rug and motioned for Alex to do the same.

Alex sat down and surprised herself with a willingness to engage with the couple, even in the darkened room. She wondered if she was beginning to trust them.

CHAPTER 24

"We brought you here so you could face the beast," Betty said, folding her hands in her lap.

"Why do I have to keep dealing with these awful things? How does this help me?"

She moved as if to push herself up from the floor but Mack grasped her arm and firmly held her in place. "It's going to be all right. I won't leave you," he said.

She surrendered to his grip, hugging her arms tightly around her knees. "So what do I have to do this time?"

"Let's begin by having you lie down," said Betty, moving closer to Alex's side. Mack arranged himself and his rug on her other side.

Alex was nervous but laid down on a large, thick blanket. To her surprise, it was comfortable and very warm.

"Good," said Betty. "Now we can begin the journey."

Mack began singing quietly, so quietly that Alex couldn't make out any recognizable words. But the song soothed her and she found herself closing her eyes and relaxing her body.

She became aware of someone touching her chest lightly. It felt pleasant and she noted the absence of the urge to open her eyes to see who it was. She found herself drifting back and thinking of the story of the priestess with the knife in her heart that Betty had told.

Mack's singing stopped and Alex listened for the dripping sounds of water but all was absolutely silent. She couldn't even hear her own breathing. As she stretched her imagination for any sound at all, she realized her sense of hearing had changed. It was as if she had entered an entirely different realm.

Releasing her need to hear anything familiar, Alex tried to open her eyes but found she could not. Panic arose and as it did, she found herself spinning as she had done days ago when Betty and Mack had appeared. She knew she could stop the spinning if she ceased trying to make it stop. As the spinning stopped, strangely, so had her panic.

She still couldn't open her eyes but now it was all right. In her mind's eye there was nothing. No pictures, no colors, no shapes. Nothing. This, combined with the absence of sound, was disconcerting but Alex merely kept her focus. She thought that if she couldn't see or hear anything, maybe she could feel something. She gingerly wiggled her fingers and was surprised that they moved.

Okay, maybe I can explore this way.

She moved her hand away from her body and explored the space around her. Still nothing.

Then suddenly, her hand made contact with something.

Instinctively, she knew it was the beast!

Her hand jerked back and now she could hear her breathing, hard and rapid. She felt sweat break out on her face and neck and all she wanted to do was to get up and run. She felt betrayed by Mack's promise that he wouldn't leave her. Then she discovered she could not move anything except her hand. She could hear the monster's breath too and wondered why it hadn't ripped her apart as it had done before.

Then she remembered when it had come to her before and she had saved herself by holding out her hands. The rainbow fire had kept him from harming her.

Now she held out her hand toward him, willing the rainbow fire to appear. She could feel its heat radiating out of her hand. Then she realized she could open her eyes at last. Although afraid to see the beast, she slowly opened first one eye and then the other.

He was there, as horrible to see as ever. But just sitting there. Looking at her. The rainbow fire seemed to be keeping him calm. She didn't know what she should do next. Slowly, Alex began to sit up.

"What you do next is embrace me. I am your brother," the beast said.

Alex was startled and withdrew her hand automatically. She realized what she had done and quickly held out the hand again, willing the fire to hold back the monster.

"There's no need for that now," he said. Although his voice was rough and deep, Alex did not sense he meant her harm.

She knew he expected her to embrace him but found she could not do it. It bumped up against every part of her carefully created survival system.

"You will reach out for me eventually, but for now an acknowledgment will suffice," he said, leaning toward her.

"I certainly acknowledge your presence here. How could I not?" Alex asked rhetorically. She looked around for Mack again. Not seeing him, she accepted her current dilemma. She recalled how resistance to Mack's and Betty's "lessons" was futile. "All right. What do you require of me?"

The beast responded by holding out a huge, hairy hand, palm up. Alex's curiosity led her to look into it. At first, she didn't recognize what she was seeing. Then, suddenly, she realized it was a miniature figure that had been torn apart. She knew it was herself.

She jerked back.

"What do you think this is?" he asked.

"It's me! When you ripped me apart and killed me!" Alex's heart was beating hard and her breath was coming in short gasps.

"But was it really you?"

"Of course it was. Or...at least it was in the dream," she replied, calming a little.

"The *real* you?" he persisted.

Alex started to reply in the affirmative, but stopped. "I'm not sure I know what the real me is."

"That's what I'm here for," said the beast. "To help you discover that 'real you'."

"But why a beast? Why not just a good psychotherapist?"

The beast snorted loudly, blowing its odorous breath at Alex. She recoiled and restated her question.

"What's the purpose of my being scared out of my wits? What good does that do?" She folded her arms across her chest and set her jaw.

"It's only necessary when nothing else has succeeded in getting your attention."

"Well, you certainly have it now," Alex replied.

CHAPTER 25

Sitting with the horrid beast, Alex couldn't imagine actually embracing him. Especially knowing how he had torn her apart in her dream. The idea that she was somehow related to him was abhorrent and unacceptable.

Interrupting her thoughts, the beast suddenly leaned toward her, once again holding out his hand with her image in it. "Take another look," he said.

"I have no intention of looking at my dead body again."

"That's why you have to look again," he said, shoving his hand closer toward her. "Look beyond merely a dead body. Look at what it can teach you."

Alex was wary, but intrigued. She cautiously leaned forward and peered into the beast's hand. This time, she didn't feel revulsion. She only felt a surprising sadness and a pressure in her chest.

Eyes beginning to tear, Alex said, "I don't understand. Why is this so important?"

"Let me show you," said the beast. "But you must trust me before I can guide you in finding the answers to your questions."

"Trust you!" Alex said. "Just why should I trust someone who killed me? Or...at least tried to." Alex was becoming confused by her complete acceptance of the experience in her dream. She had never before put so much faith in things like dreams.

"This is good. You are beginning to release your barriers. Your walls of belief are beginning to fall." The beast looked almost as if he was smiling.

"Well, they're pretty hard to maintain in the face of all I've experienced the past few days. I've either slid entirely into the world of insanity or I'm becoming the first enlightened advertising agent in America!" She let out a laugh and prepared herself for wherever it was that the beast was going to take her.

CHAPTER 26

With the fear that the beast might grab her and haul her down to an underground lair, Alex braced her body for escape.

Once again, the spinning began. By now Alex knew this was an indication that she was resisting so she set her mind to let go. The spinning stopped quickly this time.

As she refocused her eyes, the beast was no longer with her. The cave had become silent again and she sensed she was completely alone.

She felt her body relaxing and sighed with relief. *This may just be the calm before the storm so I'd better enjoy it while it lasts.*

She was correct. Her eyes became heavy and soon she had no choice but to lie down on the blanket again. But she did not fall asleep. She felt strangely alert but once again could not move. She made the decision not to try and just release into whatever was to come.

She was startled to see her advertising agency appear before her mind's eye. She saw all of her coworkers, her secretary, and her own office. She watched herself emerge from the conference room, coffee cup in one hand

and a pile of file folders in the other. She noticed her furrowed brow and look of anxiety. From what seemed to be a great distance, she heard herself barking orders to her secretary. She slowly recalled this as an event that occurred a few days before her trip to the mountains.

She remembered always fearing that if she didn't continue to land more accounts than the other agents, her promotion with the company might be in jeopardy, although no one had ever said anything to that effect. She also remembered constantly feeling angry with everyone she worked with because she believed none of them had any idea of how hard she worked.

Suddenly a picture of the beast appeared, overlaid on Alex's image. Just as suddenly, it disappeared. Then she saw her secretary, in tears, walking into her office.

"I just can't handle this anymore," Alex heard the secretary say to her. "I've really tried to get along with you, but it's like working for a...a...a monster!" The woman began wailing.

The scene faded and Alex was left shocked and disturbed at the event and her discovery of how her secretary felt about her.

"A monster? Me?" Alex found it unthinkable.

Suddenly another scene appeared. She was stuffing toast into her mouth as she yelled at her daughter. "Hurry up, Rosie, you'll be late for school!"

Alex saw Rosie's lower lip tremble and tears begin to roll from her brown eyes. "Mommy, my tummy hurts."

"Oh, great! That's all I need. Come here and let me feel your forehead," Alex heard herself say. "Okay, no fever. So get upstairs and get dressed. You cannot be late again, young lady!"

Crying, the child began climbing the stairs but turned to Alex and said, "You're like a mean old man!"

The scene faded and Alex was devastated. She remembered this interaction well. It had bothered her for days. But she hadn't done anything about it except to take Rosie, between business calls, for ice cream that weekend.

She began crying. *Oh my god, what sort of mother am I? Ice cream won't mend that precious heart.*

When her crying ceased, she replayed the scene and focused on Rosie's comment about Alex being "a mean man."

What did she mean by that? Alex asked, puzzled. Had she misunderstood her daughter? Maybe she meant "mean *mom*" rather than man.

But Alex knew Rosie had meant what she said. She knew Rosie to be incredibly insightful and intuitive, despite her youth. She had experienced her ability to accurately read someone's feelings or posturings. So she knew there was something in what Rosie had said.

All right, she said to herself, how could I be a mean *man*? She was beginning to see how Rosie, or anyone else for that matter, would think she was mean, but what was this *man* thing all about?

Again, she felt her body relax and her mind become alert. This time, however, she saw nothing in her mind's eye. She waited, expecting a picture or a scene. Instead, she heard the beast returning. Her heart raced.

"Your brother lives within you."

Upon hearing this, Alex immediately saw a picture of a powerful man. As he arrogantly strode through a group of people, he pushed them out of his way. He was dressed in an expensive suit, with hair that was perfectly styled. His face though, was hard and unyielding.

Alex was strangely fascinated. He seemed to sense her scrutiny and turned to face her. "So how am I doing so far?" he asked.

Startled, Alex stammered "What? What did you say?"

"Oh don't play coy with me, Alex. This is the job description you wrote for me a long time ago. And if I do say so myself, I've been doing very well at it," the man said, polishing his well-manicured nails on his lapel.

"What job description? I don't even know you."

The man laughed from deep within him. "Okay, so you're going to play it that way. I can deal with that. It's all part of the game anyway."

"What game? What job? What is this all about? Who *are* you anyway?"

A sense deep within her told Alex who he was. She had known it all along. She knew he was the brother Mack and Betty told her about. But not a true sibling. More a part of her that had male qualities.

"Okay, so I know you're my ... uh, 'brother,'" she said. "But what's this job description nonsense?"

"Well, if you think it's nonsense, give me another one," said the man, looking around him as if unconcerned.

"What? I never gave you one in the first place," Alex said.

"Oh? So am I to infer that I've been wasting my time protecting you all this time?" he asked.

"*Protecting* me?"

"Yes, and you certainly needed it. It's been quite a task."

"I'm perfectly capable of protecting myself," said Alex, annoyed. "And why would I need a charlatan like you to protect me?"

The man laughed uproariously. "Charlatan! That's rich. If there's anything phony about me, it's because you wanted it that way. Heaven forbid that little Alex could allow me to just be me."

Confused and annoyed but still interested in pursuing the answers she wanted, Alex persisted. "So if you're not who you seem to be, who are you? And what does it all have to do with me?"

"It has to do with you because I *am* you," said the man. "I am your masculine side, the yang to your yin, if you will."

In some popular magazine, Alex had once read about everyone having both feminine and masculine aspects within their personalities. She vaguely remembered it now.

"Fine. So I have male and female parts within me. But you're not any kind of man I'd want within me!"

"Why not?" the beast asked, laughing.

"Because you're so...so...mean!" she replied.

Alex's eyes flashed wide as she recognized what she had just said.

CHAPTER 27

Alex rubbed her eyes and sleepily opened them. Sun was streaming through the cave entrance into the interior. She looked around and, seeing no one, got up and stretched. She felt like she had slept for days. Her mouth felt fuzzy and she wanted a drink of water.

She walked toward the cave's mouth, looking around for any sign of Betty or Mack, hoping they'd have a canteen. The smell of freshly brewed coffee and something indescribably delicious wafted through the air.

"Ooh, coffee!" Alex said, running out and squatting next to Mack, who was stirring a concoction in a frying pan. "And scrambled eggs! I must have died and gone to heaven."

Mack laughed and said, "Maybe you did." Alex gave him a questioning look as she reached for the plate of eggs he offered.

"More dying?" she asked, stuffing her mouth with the most delicious eggs she'd ever eaten. "Wow! What did you put in these?"

Mack ignored her questions and offered her a tin cup of coffee that she fairly snatched from his hand.

Betty appeared, carrying a bundle of firewood and pine needles for use as tinder. "Good morning!" she called.

"So does this mean that we're not leaving this morning?" asked Alex, her fork poised midway between her plate and her mouth.

Betty just smiled at Mack and he smiled back.

"All right you two! Stop being so secretive. I know you're up to something. I feel like I'm a lone contestant on *Survivor!* You're always setting me up." Alex said, putting her unfinished plate of food down and folding her arms in front of her chest.

More laughter.

"Look, I just had a really strange experience with that beast - or man - or whoever he was supposed to be. He tried to convince me that I was him - or he was me - or some such. How ridiculous!"

"Why is that so hard to accept?" asked Mack, scraping her uneaten eggs into a plastic garbage sack. He wiped the plate and her fork with a towel and packed them away in his knapsack.

"Because he's an opportunist. He's cold and calculating and mean-hearted. He's only out for himself."

"Yes, go on," Betty said, smiling encouragingly.

"He tried to convince me I had hired him in some way - to do my bidding...to *protect* me! Can you imagine that?" Alex said, waving her hands about wildly.

"Yes, actually I can," said Betty.

Alex looked at her askance, but continued. "I know, I know. I've been a little bit too *macho* at times, but..."

Mack howled with mirth. "Macho!" he said, choking on his laughter. "That's a good one!"

Alex was encouraged. "Yeah, well, I know I could have been nicer to my secretary. But she bugs me. All the time she acts like a scared little rabbit."

The words had no sooner left her mouth than Alex saw another scene, this time for only a fleeting moment, in which her own face overlaid that of her frightened secretary.

"My god," she complained. "Now I suppose you're telling me that I'm not only a louse like that creepy guy but a wimp like my secretary as well! That's absolute crap!" Alex pulled herself up and strode off into the bushes to relieve herself.

"She's got *that* right," said Mack, throwing dirt on the campfire to extinguish the flames. Betty just smiled.

CHAPTER 28

Back in her cabin, Alex battled between her old need to escape immediately and what was now drawing her more each day. She hated facing these unpleasant revelations but knew they were somehow doing her good.

She moved to the bed and picked up the quilt's edge, playing with it in her hands. The colors had continued to become brighter and brighter as each day went by. Without knowing why, Alex took the quilt outside and spread it on the ground behind her cabin as Betty had done days earlier.

She stood, fists rammed low in the pockets of her jeans, studying the quilt. When she had her fill of one section, she would walk around for a different view.

In the patterns in the quilt, she began to see a relationship with her life. In the lower parts of the design, she saw a myriad of symbols and pictures, all haphazardly placed, some bumping into others. The pathway that ran upward over the entire quilt seemed blocked in places in the lower section. Though uncomfortable to admit, it was clear to her that this part of the quilt accurately described her life so far. It had been full of trauma, frustrations, and confusion. She was amazed that she had risen so high in her business life with all this chaos going on within her.

She squinted at something she had not noticed before. It seemed to be moving along the pathway in the lower part of the quilt. She lowered herself to a squat in order to see what this was. She assumed it was an insect crawling on the fabric.

But as her eyes adjusted, she jumped back, falling on her rump.

It was a miniature version of the beast!

"What the ...," she said, cautiously righting herself again for a better look.

She saw that wherever he went he spread more chaos over the patterns. He didn't seem to have any direction, going back and forth over the same areas. She sensed, however, that he seemed to be looking up occasionally, as if listening to something.

Alex was shocked when she heard her own voice saying loudly, "Yes, that's right, just keep going! No, I don't know which way. Just push your way through no matter what. And make sure you don't let anyone get to me!"

Get to me? She was dumbfounded by the idea.

Then it struck her. *This* is what she hadn't seen before. She had created a monstrous, macho presence within to protect her from her fears. And it had done this by overpowering and denigrating others. She suddenly understood with amazing clarity why she used the methods she had to get ahead in her business.

Most of all, she finally understood why Rosie had called her a mean man.

CHAPTER 29

Alex was devastated. Everything she had ever thought about herself was now just dust in the wind. She wished she could celebrate her new clarity but she felt as if she had been hit by a truck. A sense of betrayal haunted her and she knew she was the betrayer.

She scuffed along the dry riverbed, looking at the ground but at nothing in particular. Just walking. Thinking. Feeling great emotional pain. Her gut heaved and she fell on her knees to vomit.

When she recovered, she wiped her mouth with her sleeve. She sat on the ground, feeling its warmth. Then, for no apparent reason, looked skyward. Bright blue contrasted with small, white, fluffy clouds scudding along. They seemed happy and free. She remembered the quilt and how it depicted a similar scene of sky and clouds in its middle section. She wondered if this meant she could now move on from chaos to a peaceful period in her life.

She longed for this to be true and stayed for some time, just kneeling in the sand.

When she looked up again into the sky, she did something she didn't think she had ever done before.

She prayed.

CHAPTER 30

"Our work with you is done," said Betty, who was standing on the porch with Mack. She touched his arm affectionately and he nodded.

"What? You're leaving me? I thought we had just begun," Alex wailed.

"We had. But that's all we can do for you right now," said Mack, adjusting the strap on his knapsack. It looked full and heavy.

"It's time for you to go home," said Betty.

"Home?" said Alex, feeling misery enfold her again. "I don't feel capable of driving, let alone dealing with everything at home."

"You'll be fine," said Mack, reaching out to ruffle her hair.

"But how do I reach you if I need you?" asked Alex.

"We'll know if you do," said Betty.

Alex felt she had to accept that. "I just don't know what will happen when I get home." She hung her head and shook it slowly from side to side.

"That's good. None of this would have been worthwhile if you knew what to expect in your new life. No one knows what will happen when they've just been born," said Betty.

"Is that what I am? A newborn?" Alex tried feebly to laugh.

Betty and Mack just smiled.

"You'll be fine," they both said.

Betty walked over to the bed and picked up the quilt. Carefully and with a great deal of love, she folded it. She walked over to Alex and handed it to her.

"Don't forget your quilt," she said. Alex thought she saw the slightest moisture in Betty's eyes.

"*My* quilt?" asked Alex, eyes widening with disbelief.

"Of course it's yours. Who else would it belong to?" asked Betty.

"But I don't know what the upper section means yet," said Alex, trying to buy time.

"It's not time for you to know," said Mack. He turned to go.

"No, wait!" said Alex.

She moved across the room and flung her arms around him. He hugged her back.

As Mack released their embrace and walked out of the door, Alex could only look at Betty, wordless.

Betty said softly, "You'll be fine."

As she watched Betty and Mack get into their car and drive away, Alex reached up to smooth back her hair.

That's when she found the flower Mack had put there.

CHAPTER 31

Keys and suitcase still in hand, Alex just stood looking around her apartment. She felt rather numb and uncertain whether or not she was happy to be back. Her thoughts were muddled and she wasn't sure what she should do.

She decided that closing the door and putting her things down would be a good start. As she crossed the room toward the sliding glass door that overlooked the park, she wondered about what she had just experienced in the mountains with Betty and Mack. She tried to imagine where they were and what they were doing. She shook her head as if waking herself from a dream.

"I've got to pull myself back," she said aloud. "I can't afford to live in a fantasy world anymore. That was just a vacation. A very strange one."

Alex picked up the phone to call her office, looked at the receiver, and put it down again. Unsure if that was what she wanted to do, she decided to unpack first.

Alex jumped as the telephone began ringing. It had never sounded so loud before. As she picked up the extension by her bed, she heard the warm voice of her ex-husband.

"Hey! You're home. Did you have a good time?" David asked, sounding too enthusiastic for her present state of mind.

"How's Rosie?" she asked, wanting to avoid details of her odd adventures.

David replied, immediately recognizing her reluctance to make small talk. "She's fine. Her last day at camp is tomorrow. She wants us both to pick her up."

"*Both* of us?" Alex asked, knowing full well why Rosie would want both her parents to welcome her after being away at summer camp. "Well, I guess that would work. I'm not going into the office until Monday."

"Okay then, I'll pick you up at ten and we'll drive out to the lake," David said. Hesitating, he added, "Maybe we can even get a bite to eat at that cafe you always liked."

"Umm, maybe," Alex said, not wanting to commit. "I'll see you then."

As she hung up the phone, she paused to notice the quilt that she had unpacked and spread across her bed. The colors were brighter than ever.

CHAPTER 32

As they sped along the curving highway, David made occasional comments about the mountain scenery. Alex responded absentmindedly, keeping her head turned toward her window. She hoped he wouldn't ask anything about her trip.

"I need to get gas," he said, pulling into a small station and stepping out of the car. "Do you want anything? Soda? Snack? Anything?" He smiled as he leaned back into the driver's side window.

"Oh, no, thanks. I'm fine," Alex said. She tried to give him an authentic smile but they both knew it was forced.

David pumped the gas and paid the attendant. As he pulled back onto the road, he cleared his throat.

"You seem quiet."

"I do?" asked Alex, trying to be casual. "It's just so beautiful up here. I'm enjoying the trees."

"Uh-huh," said David. "You just seem to have something on your mind. You're not your usual self."

Alex peered at him askance. "What is my 'usual' self?"

"Well, you know. Talkative. About your work."

"Oh. That," Alex replied, turning her head once more toward the window.

"*That*?" asked David, slowing the car and turning his head toward her. "Sounds funny hearing you downplay your work."

"I'm not downplaying anything," Alex said. "I just don't think you need to know everything about my life, that's all." She sat up straighter and fussed with her blouse as if it was suddenly several sizes too small.

"Oops, sorry," David said. He sounded sincere and Alex was sorry she had snapped at him.

They drove along in silence for several miles. Alex began to feel drowsy and laid her head on the neck rest, closing her eyes. As she drifted off, lulled by the hum of the engine, she saw images of the mountains and the cabin she'd stayed in. Releasing herself totally into relaxation, she was abruptly awakened by Mack's voice in her ear.

"What did your brother teach you?" the voice said.

Alex's eyes flew open and her body jolted.

"What's wrong?" asked David. "Are you okay?" He slowed the car and pulled over to the side.

Cutting the engine, he turned to Alex. Her face was blanched and her body was shaking, so he reached over to her and took her hand in both of his.

"Alex, what on earth is going on?"

She took a long look at him. His obvious and genuine concern triggered a burst of sobs. David pulled her over toward him and enclosed her in his arms, stroking her hair.

"Talk to me," he said.

Alex pulled away and looked into David's kind face. She could see he was deeply worried. He handed her a box of tissues from the console.

Drying her eyes and blowing her nose, Alex tried to speak. But all that came out was a gasp.

"It's okay. Take your time."

Alex's mind was churning. Not only was she mired in confusion about what had happened on her trip, but now she was terrified of the feelings emerging here with David. She remembered how he had always encouraged her to talk to him about anything. And she knew how she had always pushed him away, never really sharing her thoughts and feelings with him.

Now, she felt so weakened and vulnerable, there was nothing standing in the way of telling him everything.

CHAPTER 33

"Come on, let's take the car robe and sit over there on that rock wall," David said, helping her out of the car.

Alex was still shaky so he put his arm firmly around her waist as they walked over to the viewpoint. He spread the blanket on the low wall and they swung their legs over it so they could sit with their backs to the road and face the lovely view of distant mountains.

For several minutes they sat in silence, just gazing at purple-colored mountains. Pointing towards them, Alex finally spoke.

"That's where I was. Well, maybe not those particular mountains, but in the mountains." She paused.

"Yes. Go on," said David.

"I don't know how to describe what happened there. To me. It's still happening." Alex was stumbling, trying to make her words make sense. "Oh I know this is stupid!" She started to get up but David restrained her with a light touch.

She looked at him and decided to continue. She cleared her throat and wiped at her nose.

"I met some very strange people up there," she began.

CHAPTER 34

Savoring her burger, Alex had never tasted anything so good. She felt the sun warming her cheek through the cafe window. David's presence was just as comforting.

"Boy," she said, stuffing her mouth with fries that she had dipped into dollops of catsup, "I sure unloaded on you."

"You needed to talk," David said. His turkey on rye was sitting half eaten on the plate he had pushed away earlier. He sipped his iced tea, watching her through his intensely blue eyes.

Now it was Alex's turn to be concerned about David. He had been exceedingly quiet as they drove to the cafe as well as during their meal. She was convinced she had made a grave mistake in telling him about her bizarre adventures.

"Now you know why I never wanted to talk much when we were married," said Alex. "I was probably worried that you'd think you'd married a nut case!" Her attempt at humor failed when she saw David's unsmiling face.

"I'm sorry," she said. "I should have kept it all to myself. Please just forget it. Who knows, it may not even have happened. I was just really stressed out and I..."

"Stop, Alex," David said, putting his tea down with a clunk. "You needn't apologize. I admit what you told me is pretty difficult to take in, but you're not a 'nut case,' as you say it. I'm not a psychologist, but I would say you've had an extraordinary experience. And I mean *extra*-ordinary - like, out of the ordinary. I believe these things happen even though I can't explain them."

Alex deeply appreciated his words and the sincerity behind them. "I wish you could," she said, leaning toward him over the table between them.

"Well," said David, smiling for the first time since they left the viewpoint. "Maybe we can figure it out together.

CHAPTER 35

"Mommy! Daddy! You both came!" shrieked Rosie, throwing herself at Alex and David.

"Whoa, Munchkin," said David, swinging her up into his arms. "You've gotten so strong here at camp you almost knocked me down!"

Alex reached to take Rosie from David and gave her daughter a long, lingering hug. She felt David's warm hand on her back and liked it.

Loading Rosie's gear into the car, the little girl cautioned them to be careful of the mysterious package that stuck out of the top of her backpack.

"Don't break it, Daddy! And don't look at it! It's a surprise for when we get home," Rosie said, jumping up and down. Her sneakers were filthy, but her little round, suntanned face was beaming.

"Okay, I'll watch it," said David, closing the trunk carefully over the pack. He helped her into her seat restraint in the back seat and slid behind the wheel.

On their way back to the city, Rosie chattered nonstop about all her adventures in camp, including the time she had to throw up because she had eaten too many "s'mores."

"Annie, you know, my camp counselor, she helped me change my pajamas because they smelled bad. She told me you could wash them when I got home but I told her you'd be mad and just throw them out," Rosie said to Alex.

Alex was shocked. *My god. Here it is again. My daughter thinks I'm the "mean man."*

"Rosie, I'm not mad and I'm not going to throw your pajamas away."

Rosie's eyes widened. "You're not? You mean I can keep them?" She seemed innocently delighted at the revelation. "They're my favorites. They're my Harry Potter ones."

Alex reassured her again and turned back around to face the road.

I've got some big time work to do! she told herself.

In her mind's eye she saw - or thought she saw - Betty, smiling at her.

CHAPTER 36

David pulled up in front of Alex's apartment building, cut the motor and stepped out to gather Rosie's things from the trunk. Rosie popped out of her seat restraint and held Alex's hand as they waited for David.

"Thanks for driving," Alex said to David.

"You're not getting rid of me yet," he said, smiling down at Rosie.

"Yay! Daddy's staying, Daddy's staying!" Rosie shouted.

David looked at Alex questioningly. Alex felt torn between wanting him to go and wanting him to stay. She felt anxious about having shared so much with him and now wanted to forget she had even spoken about her experiences on the mountain.

"Well," she said, looking at Rosie, then at David. "I guess for just a little while."

Rosie grabbed her father's hand with her free one and pulled them all merrily into the building.

Rosie ran off to her bedroom to unpack and David asked Alex if he should go. He seemed to be feeling uncomfortable now that he was in Alex's domain.

"Oh. No. I guess you can stay," said Alex, also feeling nervous.

David tried to ease the discomfort by laughing. "Wow. That's a real welcoming invitation."

"I'm sorry. I just don't know what I'm feeling right now," said Alex. "Why don't you sit down? I'll make us some iced tea. You didn't get to finish yours at the cafe."

"That would be nice," he said, sounding relieved.

Alex called from the kitchen. "We didn't even talk about you. How's your life been lately? How's your work? Have you sold any paintings?"

"Yes, actually I've had a pretty nice commission from the Arthur Foundation. They've asked me to design a large mural for their new D.C. offices."

"David! That's fabulous!" said Alex, coming around the breakfast bar to serve him the tea. "It's about time that your talent is fully recognized."

She stood smiling down at him, holding his tea and hers. As their eyes met, David reached up, removed the glasses from her hands and placed them on the coffee table. He took her hands in his and gently pulled her down next to him on the sofa.

"So you recognize talent when you see it, do you?" he asked, pushing back an unruly strand of her hair from her face.

"Why don't we see what else I might excel in, shall we?" David said as he leaned forward to kiss her.

CHAPTER 37

Alex awoke to Rosie's insistent banging and rattling of her bedroom door. "Mommy! Are you still sleeping? I want to have breakfast with you," the girl shouted.

Rubbing her eyes, Alex looked at the clock on the bed stand. It was indeed time for breakfast and as she moved to get out of bed, she bumped into an arm.

She jumped. "Oh no!" She leapt away and saw David's tousled blondish hair emerging from the covers. Just awakened, he wore a sleepy smile on his face.

"You've got to get out of here," she said, looking around feverishly for his clothes. She spied them on the floor and threw them onto the bed. Then she realized her own state of undress and frantically grabbed a blanket to cover herself. She felt frozen to the spot and couldn't find anything else to say. She was terrified.

David saw her confusion and fear and rose to a sitting position. "Hold on, Alex. Just calm down. It's okay. Rosie won't be shocked. She won't mind," he said.

"Won't mind?" Alex said with a shriek. "Of course she won't mind. What you're not understanding is that she'll think we're back together!"

"And aren't we?" David asked, slowly getting out of bed and moving toward Alex.

"Stop! Don't come any closer," said Alex, backing away. "We're not going to do this!"

David bent to pull on his boxers and said quietly, "Just what are you afraid of us doing?"

"This!" she replied, waving her hand around the room.

"Messing up your bedroom, you mean?" said David, in an unsuccessful bid for humor.

"Don't be an ass!" Alex said. "You know what I mean. We're divorced in case you'd forgotten. Don't you remember why we got divorced?"

"Actually, no, I don't," David said as he pulled on pants and shirt. "Although I think it had something to do with your not wanting to share your life with me, not liking to communicate feelings with me."

She knew she was being set up. "So now that I foolishly told you everything that happened with Betty and Mack, you think we can get back together? Well, if that's what you think, you've got another thing coming!"

David grinned as he left the room. "Oh, I'll look forward to that."

Alex watched, stunned, as he swung Rosie into his arms.

"Let's you and me fix Mom a big pancake breakfast," David told the beaming girl.

"Cool!" said Rosie. "Then I can give you the present I made for you and Mommy! I can't wait for you to see it. It's a popcorn bowl that I made in pottery class. You're going to love it!"

As he turned to take Rosie into the kitchen, he flashed Alex his crossed-eye, tongue-out, goofy look that she had always hated when they were married.

She had to work hard now not to laugh.

CHAPTER 38

On Monday morning, Alex walked into her office an hour earlier than she was expected. She had hoped to avoid having to talk to anyone. She just wanted to catch up on the work she had missed while she was gone, make some necessary phone calls, and generally immerse herself so deeply that no one would dare bother her.

But her plans were cut short when she saw her secretary, Eileen, sitting at her desk, typing furiously.

Alex cleared her throat and adjusted her jacket.

"Oh, good morning, Eileen. What are you doing here so early?"

Eileen looked aghast when she heard Alex's voice. She stopped what she had been typing into her computer and selected "sleep" from its menu. The screen went dark.

Alex suspected Eileen had been using the office system for personal use, which was against policy, and felt slightly irritated.

Choosing not to make an issue of it, Alex excused herself, explaining to Eileen that she had to dig in and wouldn't be available to anyone who called or came in. She wondered at Eileen's strange expression.

In her office, Alex looked at the stacks of papers, reports and account books. She sighed with a feeling bordering on despair. This surprised her and she had to admit that she dreaded getting back to the old routine.

Shaking herself loose from such dangerous thoughts, she sat down and began going through the latest stack. She lost her sense of time and when Eileen quietly entered her office and dropped a sheet of paper on her desk, she was jolted.

"Oh, Eileen. You startled me."

"Uh, oh. I only wanted to leave this," Eileen said, pointing to the paper. She looked red-faced and frightened.

"What is it?" asked Alex, reaching to pick it up.

"It's...uh...well...I..." stammered Eileen, turning as if to leave the office.

"No, wait. Let's see what it is. If I need to respond to it..." Alex began. She stopped herself when she realized it was a letter of resignation from Eileen.

"Eileen! What does this mean? You're quitting?"

"Yes, ma'am," said Eileen, wringing her hands in front of her skirt. "I, uh, I have to take care of my mother. You know, I've told you she's been sick."

Alex knew Eileen was lying. A surge of anger started to rise but it melted almost as quickly as it had appeared. In its place was a need to understand.

"Eileen. Sit down, would you?" Alex said, suggesting the nearby chair with her hand. "Please." She smiled at the young woman.

Eileen cautiously sat on the edge of the chair, still wringing her hands. "There's really nothing to talk about, Ms. Wilder. I've made up my mind. My mother needs me."

Alex came around from behind the desk, almost leaned against it to speak with Eileen, then decided against it. She chose instead to sit in another chair, closer to her secretary and on eye level.

Eileen's suspicion grew. She backed further into her chair. Alex sensed she was shaking.

Without knowing why, Alex put her hand gently on Eileen's knee. "Eileen, we both know you don't have to take care of your mother."

Eileen looked shocked, then fearful. She started to speak, but Alex cut her off.

"Look. I've known for a long time you haven't been happy here." Eileen started to protest but Alex once again waved her off. "I haven't been the easiest boss to work for."

The young woman's expression changed from fear to utter surprise. Her eyebrows rose and her mouth dropped open.

"Ms. Wilder, I don't know what to say," she said, her trembling now abating.

"You don't have to say anything, Eileen. It's me that has much to say. For now, I just want to ask you to stay. You've been an efficient and trustworthy assistant," said Alex.

On the word, "assistant," Eileen's eyebrows rose even higher.

Alex laughed. "Yes, I said 'assistant.' How would you like a promotion from secretary to 'Administrative Assistant?'"

Eileen burst into tears. Her obvious relief and surprise written all over her. She stood up, wiping at her eyes. "Ms. Wilder, what's happened to you?"

As Alex stood to embrace Eileen, she laughed quietly. "Let's just say the monster doesn't work here anymore."

As she left Alex's office in wonder, Eileen ran a hand through her curly blond hair and felt like she had just visited another planet.

CHAPTER 39

"Good night, Ms. Wilder...and thanks again," called Eileen.

"Good night, Eileen. See you tomorrow. Oh, and Eileen...have a good evening."

Alex turned her leather swivel chair to look out of the large window behind her desk. Lights of the city twinkled and she realized how late she had worked that day. But something had changed. Ordinarily at this time she would be wound up like a watch spring, feeling vague anxiety and pressure that she hadn't accomplished enough.

Now, however, she leaned back in her chair, laced her fingers together over her abdomen, and felt satisfied. Strange feeling, that satisfaction. She mused that she might never have felt it before. She considered what she had done that day, knew there was much unfinished work, but felt fine anyway.

The difference she was experiencing was about how she had spent her day, not how much she had done. She recalled how she had lingered at the coffee machine with a coworker, just chatting about their children. Later, she had popped her head into her boss's office just to say hello and ask after his wife, who had recently had surgery for gallstones. She had laughed to herself as she walked away at the shocked and confused look on his face.

Now, as she gazed out over the city, she wondered where her life was going to lead her. Before, she had always known because she had a well-defined plan. But she didn't feel the need for one any longer. At least not the same plan. Her prime objective now revolved around reestablishing her relationship with Rosie.

And maybe, just maybe, it might involve making some changes around here.

Alex smiled broadly as she walked to the elevator.

"Life is good!" she said, giving a little skip, then looking furtively around to see if anyone had seen.

CHAPTER 40

Rosie shrieked with delight as she bolted toward Alex.

"Mommy! You're home early! We haven't even had our bedtime story yet!" she said, snuggling into Alex's arms.

Early! Have I really missed so many bedtime stories?

"Do you want me to stay, Ms. Wilder? Will you be going out again?" asked Millie, Alex's babysitter.

Shocked once more at what she had been doing for so long, Alex shook her head.

"No, thanks, Millie. And actually, I won't be needing you to pick Rosie up from after-school daycare anymore. I'll be doing that myself."

Millie's face registered great surprise, then beamed. The fifty-something woman looked at Alex for several moments, then spoke.

"I'm so glad, Ms. Wilder. Rosie deserves a mother."

As she closed the door after Millie, Alex just leaned against it.

Seems like everyone saw what I was doing except me.

Alex walked into the kitchen to warm some milk.

"Put your pj's on, sweetie. I'll be in there to read you a story in just a minute. I'm making us some hot cocoa," Alex called through to the bedroom.

As she watched the milk simmer, she realized that her behavior with Rosie and with Eileen might only be the tip of the proverbial iceberg. She wondered what else she had been doing unawares. Turning off the flame on the burner, Alex poured the steaming milk into two mugs and stirred in extra spoonfuls of cocoa mix.

She sighed as she put the mugs on a tray and carried it down the hallway to Rosie's room.

All this just because I had a bad dream! What could possibly be next?

CHAPTER 41

"Alex, will you please step into my office?" Mr. Billings had a curious look on his face.

Feeling surprisingly free of anxiety, Alex smiled and motioned to her boss that she would be there momentarily. She completed her call to one of her clients and put the receiver into its cradle.

Walking to Mr. Billings' office, Alex felt light-footed and happy. She thought it strange that her attention should be on the bright sunny day outside instead of what her boss was about to say to her. For all she knew, he could be announcing her termination.

And I really don't care if he does!

Mr. Billings' secretary's face contorted with scorn as Alex let out a giggle.

"Uh, Mr. Billings wanted to see me," said Alex, finding it difficult to stifle yet another giggle at the look on the woman's face.

"Yes, Ms. Wilder. Go right in." Madge wore a thin smile of superiority as she conjectured the same possibility that Alex was going to be fired.

"Sit down, Alex." Mr. Billings motioned her to a chair in front of his desk. "First I want to thank you for your concern about my wife. I wasn't aware that you knew about her surgery. She's doing fine."

He got up and walked around his desk to stand in front of the window. Appearing to be interested in what was outside, Ralph Billings seemed uncomfortable.

Here it comes, thought Alex. *Oh well, it's his loss.* She laughed silently to herself at her calmness.

"How long have you been working here, Alex?"

"Seven years, Mr. Billings." Alex rose slightly in her seat to see what could possibly be holding his attention outside. *Maybe he sees Betty's car!*

The man spun around as Alex's laugh burst from her mouth.

"I'm sorry," she said, trying to compose herself.

Ralph Billings leaned his back against the window and folded his arms across his chest.

"Are you happy with your job here?"

Surprised, Alex searched for an answer but found it difficult because everything in her life had changed so drastically. And since the weeks after her return, those changes had expanded into all areas of her life. Feelings of freedom and hope for a meaningful future were common now.

"That's okay. Don't bother constructing an answer. I know you haven't been satisfied with your work." He looked down at his feet, which were shifting backward and forward.

Alex was confused at where he was going with all of this. *Strange way to terminate someone.*

"Mr. Billings," she said, venturing into potentially dangerous territory, "it's not that I haven't been satisfied. It's just that I've had some changes in my life recently and they're affecting me deeply. I'm sorry if I'm not living up to your expectations any longer." She thought she would give him a more comfortable route to his difficult task.

"You're not catching my drift, Alex," he replied. "It's more that you weren't living up to my expectations *before*."

Alex's eyes widened in surprise.

"I had been considering letting you go," Billings continued. "But over the past few weeks, I've noticed a difference. I can't quite put my finger on what it is. But I like it. Very much." He smiled and uncrossed his arms, putting his hands on the window sill behind him and leaning forward.

Alex was speechless. She had been convinced that he had made the final decision to fire her at the last staff meeting. She had been outspoken about an account for a company whose stated purpose was to share profits with the less fortunate members of their surrounding community. Their activities had included holding street fairs to assist local artists and distributing baskets of food to the needy. All the other ad executives wanted to let the account go because it wasn't bringing in enough revenue. Alex had fought to keep them as clients and offered to take responsibility for the promotional work they needed in order to stay in business and serve the community. She had even offered to accept a reduction in her commission. Some of the other execs had laughed because they thought she was kidding. Others sneered and made comments about her being a new millennium hippy.

"Alex, I never told you this but I've had a dream for a very long time," Billings said, looking over her head as if in a reverie. "I always wanted to do something for others but got caught up early in this rat race." He motioned with his hand around the office.

Alex's interest was aroused but she had no idea that what he was about to say would affect her life profoundly.

CHAPTER 42

"David!" Alex nearly shouted into the receiver. "You'll never guess what just happened!"

"Tell me," David replied, motioning to the art student who was trying to ask a question that he'd talk to her later. The girl frowned and turned on her heel. David got up and walked with his cell phone into the hallway. "There, now I can hear you. What happened?"

"It's my job!"

"You quit?" asked David, smiling broadly.

"No, you ninny, I got promoted!"

David's response was silence.

"David? David? Are you still there?" Alex was slightly irritated because she knew why he wasn't responding. He had always wanted her to ease up on the intensity of her job's responsibilities - or at least what she thought were her responsibilities. "You need to hear about this," she insisted.

"All right, I'm listening," said David, cautiously.

"The promotion - it's not what you think," she continued. She was literally jumping in her seat. She stood up to calm herself so she could focus on what she was telling him.

"So what is it?"

"Well, it's new. It's sort of experimental," Alex said. "We - Mr. Billings and I - are taking a real risk on this one."

"I have no idea what you're talking about," said David. He suspected she was just trying to soften him up.

"I know, I know," she said. "Let's meet for dinner and I'll explain then."

"That's fine," said David. "But don't make me wait until then to find out just what this 'risk' is."

"Well," said Alex, "I think I've just jumped off a cliff."

CHAPTER 43

The persistent ringing of the phone jarred Alex out of a deep sleep. She moaned and felt for the receiver.

"What," she said, pulling herself up to a sitting position.

"Is this Alex Wilder?"

"Yes...who is this please?" Alex did not recognize the voice.

"Jim Buckingham. Of Buckingham Products. We're one of your accounts."

"Oh, yes. But how did you get my home phone number?" Now fully awake, she wrestled on her robe and walked into the kitchen, balancing the phone on her left shoulder. As she put the tea kettle on the burner, she noted a hesitation on the line.

"Hello?" she said, wondering if he had hung up.

"I'm here," he said. "Ralph Billings gave me your number. He said he knew you wouldn't mind."

Well, Ralph was wrong! "What is it you want?" Alex asked, choosing a tea bag from the container and dipping it into the mug of hot water. She tried to sound polite but was irritated at her boss's presumptuousness.

"I didn't want to talk about this while you were at work."

"Talk about what, Mr. Buckingham?" Again, she tried to sound courteous.

"Well, I might as well start at the beginning. Do you have a few minutes?"

Without waiting for her to reply, the man began.

"I'm a veteran of the Viet Nam war. While I was there, I became involved with a village near our main base camp. There were many children in this particular village and I found myself coordinating a relief effort for them. You know, asking friends in the states to send over clothing and other essentials. We collected money from the other soldiers to buy food for them. They had been farmers but the war curtailed their livelihood. They were close to starving, although the kids had been begging and even stealing in order that their families could eat and survive."

Alex had found a comfortable spot on her sofa where she now sat, curled up with her legs under her. She rested her tea cup on the arm of the couch and listened.

"Well, that was a turning point in my life and I vowed to never forget how important it is to take care of others. When I got home, I was swept up in finishing my education - I had been in an M.B.A. program before I got drafted. I got married, had kids, bought the house and the two cars - you know, the dog and all that."

Alex was beginning to be intrigued by this man's story because she could so easily relate to it.

"It was only after a strange event that my life took me back to remembering my vow," Jim said. Then he waited.

"Go on," she said.

"Uh...I don't quite know how to say this," he said, clearing his throat. He was obviously uncomfortable.

"I've had some pretty strange experiences too, so I'm listening," Alex said with a smile.

"Well, first I have to tell you that I lied."

"What? What about?" Alex frowned, fearing she had been taken in.

"Ralph wasn't the one who gave me your number."

Silence.

"Well...who then? Who gave it to you?" Alex was beginning to sense the return of the strange feelings she had learned to know so well in her adventures in the mountains.

"Mack."

Alex jolted so wildly that her mug of tea went flying and crashed onto the hardwood floor, spilling its contents.

"What?" she said. "In all these months we've been working on your account together, you never mentioned that you knew him."

"It's not the kind of thing one talks about in a typical business atmosphere," he said. "I knew from Ralph that you were in charge of working with businesses such as mine in a non-traditional way, but I had to get to know you a bit better before I revealed my connection to Mack and Betty."

"Just what *is* your connection to them?" Alex felt herself being protective of her unusual friends.

"They helped me remember my vow," he replied.

"How did they do that?" She was testing him now.

He laughed. "I understand your suspicion of this. I might be too if someone had waked me up with strange stories."

The tension broke as Alex laughed too. As she settled back into the soft couch, she said, "I'm no stranger to 'strange.' Go on with your story."

CHAPTER 44

After dropping Rosie off at school, Alex drove through heavy traffic thinking about what Jim Buckingham had told her that morning. His story was similar to hers in how Mack and Betty had shown up just at the point where he had lost conscious awareness of where his life was leading. He told her that he had thought he was happy and satisfied but his experiences with the two of them had opened him to a whole new reality. He described it as being a "reality of reality." She liked that because it so aptly portrayed her increasing familiarity with a more meaningful existence.

The result of their conversation lead them to a new level of acceptance and enthusiasm about their dedication to turning an ordinary business relationship into one that would serve many, rather than just those who would benefit monetarily. Jim had described how his previous promotional activities of Buckingham Products had always fit the normal advertising hype modes. Simply, its purpose was to pad his pockets as well as those of the other higher level employees. After his experiences with Betty and Mack, however, his intention had done a one-eighty. He had restructured the mission of his entire business, changing priorities and even letting some executives go who could not share his vision. The employees who chose to stay loved the new profit sharing, flexible hours, and childcare center now established at Buckingham Products. Jim had even enlisted his wife and two teenaged daughters to paint lively colors and designs on the walls of the community room, which had previously been an austere, colorless lunch room.

But his favorite part of the business now was the "Giving Hands" program he had fathered. It was now in the capable hands of his assistant, whose full-time job was to administer the program. He loved not having to deal with the details, which allowed him to actually interact with the people his company was helping. His favorite Saturday activity was rolling up his sleeves to help build a community garden or rebuild someone's garage into a vibrant and productive workshop. He and his family had even moved from their posh upper crust neighborhood into the one they were sponsoring. Two other employees followed suit and before long, the old, rundown section of six square blocks was blossoming - and so were its residents.

Alex enjoyed mulling these ideas over. She was so happy her boss had given her the opportunity to work with people like Jim. She felt, as Buckingham did, that her life had taken on new meaning.

Before they ended their conversation that morning, they had agreed to meet for lunch at the community center in Jim's neighborhood. She had been there before, but never with so clear a purpose. They had agreed to explore the next step for "Giving Hands." She would find out only later what that next step really meant.

CHAPTER 45

"I just read your letter and I want you to know that I'm concerned about you."

"There's nothing to be concerned about, Mother. Everything is fine. I wouldn't have written to you if it wasn't," said Alex, trying to be patient.

"Oh, so that means when you're in trouble, you won't let me know?"

Exasperated, Alex took a deep breath. "That's not what I said, Mother. I wrote to you because I thought you'd like to share in the good things that are happening in my life."

"Well," said the woman huffily. "It didn't sound too good to me. All this working with homeless people. You can never be too careful with that kind."

In times past, her mother's criticisms would have blown Alex sky-high with rage. She would have written her mother off for another few years, only reconnecting when she thought enough time had passed that maybe, just maybe, they could have a decent conversation.

As she concluded the call and hung up, she thought about how her mother was just who she was, that she would probably never change, and that Alex would just have to accept her. Strangely, she felt fine about that. Certainly, there was a sadness that she would never be able to connect deeply with her mother, but she knew that it wasn't the point of the relationship.

From her mother, she had learned to be strong and independent, not because the woman had been a good role model for these things, but precisely because she hadn't. Alex had had to learn to be self-reliant because no one else in the household was. Her father had relinquished any power he might have had to her mother, who misused hers by manipulating family members. Alex had always felt something wasn't right about all of this and had struck out on her own at an early age.

When her parents told her they would only pay for her college education if she lived at home, she told them in no uncertain terms that she was moving out. She got a job and paid her own way through college and shared a cheap apartment with a gay roommate. His name was Brian and his bizarre sense of humor provided comic relief for the years of colorless existence with her family. She and Brian had become very close, sharing stories of their lovers, but they lost contact after college graduation. She had last heard that he was living in Africa with a boyfriend who was doing some kind of work for an American ambassador.

Now, after her experiences of the past few months, Alex felt differently about many things, including her relationship with her mother. Somehow, she was becoming grateful that her mother had helped her become independent by the mere fact of her ineffectiveness as a role model. Alex thought it was strange but true that her mother had been an adversary, at times even an enemy, but the tension of that had contributed greatly to her ability to strike out in the world on her own. She knew her relationship with her mother had affected her own relationship with Rosie, although up until recently, she had believed her parenting of the little girl was the antithesis of how her mother had raised her. She realized now that even though it had *seemed* to be different from the way her mother dealt with her, its foundations were most likely based upon the same fears that her mother had. She and her mother had just chosen different ways to disguise their deep insecurities. Lately she had begun to realize that it took greater courage to express feelings, as she was now doing with Rosie, than to hide them.

As she mulled all of this over in her mind, she felt a bubble of excitement rise in her chest.

Life's not perfect...but it's good!

CHAPTER 46

Jim reached out a big warm hand to greet her warmly. He guided her to what he was referring to these days as his "office." It was the community garden, where Alex saw several people digging, planting and weeding various beds, which consisted of various types of vegetables and flowers. It was lovely. A little boy was helping his mother push markers into the ground that signified the names of each vegetable.

"Oh, this is wonderful! I'm so glad you invited me out here," said Alex, turning around to get a complete view of the space. "When I was here before, this was only a vacant lot."

"More like a vacant junk pile," said Jim, laughing. He picked up a rake that was lying on the pathway, tines up, and leaned it safely against a wall. "Come on, let me introduce you to someone."

Around the corner, the garden pathway ended and the junk pile reappeared. It was evident that this was still a work in progress. In the middle of a stack of old rusted pipes and rotting boards was an elderly man in a wheelchair. As they approached him, he turned. Alex observed his Asian face and was struck by the radiance of his eyes. They glittered. He didn't smile but it wasn't needed. Alex felt as if she had known him for a long time.

As she put out her hand to take his, Jim told her the man's name was Tam Tuyen.

"Tam is from Viet Nam. I met him and his family when I was there," Jim explained. "When the war ended, Tam's family had either been killed or died of disease. So I pulled some strings and brought him here."

"I'm happy to meet you, Tam," Alex said. The man was still holding her hand and looking deeply into her eyes. The intensity of his eyes reminded her of those of Mack's and Betty's. She laughed out loud, then checked herself, thinking it would be misunderstood.

"Don't give up your laughter," said Tam. "Americans don't laugh enough - at least not at the right things."

All three chuckled in agreement.

Jim described how invaluable Tam was in the garden project because he came from a long line of farmers in his Vietnamese family. His skills were uncanny and he was known among the people in the neighborhood as "The Alchemist" because it seemed that his "potions" that he added to the plants made them grow faster and more productively than anything they had ever known. He had a particular knack for growing larger than ordinary lemons and would often laugh uproariously when someone peeled one, popped a succulent slice into their mouth, only to realize it was not a grapefruit.

Two youths approached Tam and waited politely until Jim had finished talking to him. Then the boys asked the elder what he needed them to do. As he began listing instructions, Jim waved a goodbye and Alex followed suit, although she inwardly felt that bowing might be more appropriate. She sensed she had been in the presence of a true teacher.

CHAPTER 47

"I wanted you to meet Tam so you could get a better sense of what we are doing here and what is possible," said Jim, pouring two mugs of hot coffee and handing one to Alex. The small building in which they stood served as an office for the project and was adjacent to the garden.

"Thanks," she said, sipping the steaming liquid. "I think I am getting the idea. This project of yours is more than just your own, isn't it?" She looked directly into his smiling face.

"You got it!" he said. "I've been approached by a few people over the past couple of years to share our secrets. The funny thing is, other than Tam's potions, which he doesn't share with anyone, we have no secrets. What we do speaks for us. We were interviewed on Sixty Minutes about nine months ago and the response was overwhelming. That's when I asked your boss to shift the focus of the promotion work for Buckingham Products to something that would include this project. It's a model for other communities but mainly for other businesses and corporations. It has proved that to give freely to the community doesn't have to deplete revenues. Actually, ours have increased, as you probably already know."

He stirred cold water into his coffee. "Don't like burned lips," he said, laughing.

"Yes, I do know," said Alex. "But not every corporation has a Jim Buckingham - or a Tam."

"Oh, but they can have," Jim replied. "I have an idea for a training program." His smile changed. His look was mysterious.

"Uh-oh," said Alex, lowering the cup she was about to drink from. "I don't know if I like that look on your face."

"We'll see," said Jim, taking a big gulp of coffee, "we'll see."

As he turned to lead Alex out of the room, he studied her for a moment. Then he winked.

CHAPTER 48

Alex was listening intently to Tam, who was leading her though a large, lovely flower garden. He pointed out the vast varieties of plants and what they each needed to thrive and produce the largest blossoms. They passed through a trellis that was covered with a vine that held fragrant flowers. She saw huge trees that she couldn't identify because their fruit was so large.

She happily followed him through the next trellis where she saw a huge pool surrounded by a lovely rock garden. There were stone steps leading down into the pool, whose waters were deep aqua in color but seemed to change as she neared.

"This is the source of our garden," said Tam, motioning with his hand. "This water makes things grow."

"Oh, this is where you get your magic potion," said Alex.

Tam laughed a deep belly laugh.

He indicated she was to disrobe and step into the pool. She didn't hesitate and quickly found herself immersed in the surprisingly warm water. She felt the stone steps under her feet and realized they descended even deeper than she expected.

She continued her descent and found herself under the surface, but able to breath quite normally. She could see easily through the clear water and began to explore.

Immediately, Alex was swept up by a strong current and taken through what seemed to be a corridor where large framed paintings floated freely. As she focused on them, she recognized them as scenes from her life. In the back of her mind, she was thinking about the pictures that moved in the Harry Potter books that Rosie so loved. As she reflected, the scenes in the frames also began to move.

The current took her rapidly through the corridor of paintings. She discovered she was strangely able to encompass everything that was happening in the pictures, even though there were only moments between each one.

Suddenly, the current made a ninety degree turn, throwing Alex into great dizziness and disorientation. She struggled to return to normal awareness but that only increased her discomfort.

Then, remembering what she had learned from Betty and Mack about struggling only making things worse, she let go and the dizziness stopped.

Now she found herself in a room filled with people. They all seemed to be suffering greatly, although she couldn't identify the source of their pain. Most were hunched over, concentrating on their misery. As she focused on them, she saw what seemed to be after-images around their physical bodies, which were identical to the bodies except that they were ghostlike. And those ethereal images were reaching out to her as if to plead for her help.

She didn't know what to do and felt great despair. "What do you want?" she asked them.

Then she heard the voice.

"Use your hands."

CHAPTER 49

Alex waited in the small restaurant, sipping her tea. She wondered why she was, once again, calling upon David to be her confidant. She knew she had been trying to avoid something deeper that was developing between them. As she struggled to maintain a comfortable distance between them, her inner discomfort only grew.

She laughed quietly to herself. *I know, I know. Betty and Mack would just tell me to stop struggling.* She admitted to herself that that was exactly what she wanted to do. She was curious, although at least a bit frightened, of what would happen if she allowed a real intimacy to grow between herself and David. She was slightly irritated at the thought because she had been having a distinct feeling lately that David already knew what would happen. *Damn! He thinks this is all really hilarious and is just waiting for me to think so too!* Surprising herself, she smiled.

"Hi," said David, standing next to the booth.

Alex jumped. "You rat! How long have you been standing there?"

"Long enough," he said, sliding into the seat opposite her. "What's up?"

She eyed him, suspicious of his casual manner. Then she reminded herself of her vow to let the walls tumble. In the same moment, she felt an inner quickening as she allowed herself to admit how handsome he was.

Smiling, she waved for the waitress to get her mind off his well-built physique.

"Thought you might like some coffee or something before I start."

Her smile broadened as she saw his reaction to this. She felt a deep satisfaction in his looking very unsure of what she would tell him. *Gotcha! Maybe I'll let him sweat a bit!*

She began talking about the weather and enjoyed every bit of his growing irritation. The waitress brought coffee and stood waiting for his order, pad in hand and shifting her weight from foot to foot.

"Coffee's fine for now," he said. The woman shuffled off while sliding her pencil down the neck of her uniform, ostensibly to scratch something that itched.

Alex grinned as she recalled the cook at the diner and wondered if he and the waitress were related.

"All right. Enough about the weather. What's this meeting all about?"

Alex had teased him enough. "Well, not exactly a meeting," she said. "That sounds so businesslike."

"Fine. Not a meeting. What's whatever this is about?" He was on the verge of being annoyed.

"David, why are you so upset? It seems like you think you know what I'm going to say and that it's not going to be something you want to hear."

His mouth dropped open for a split second. He put down his coffee, and took a deep breath.

"I'm sorry. You're probably right. All the way over here I kept thinking you were going to tell me we couldn't keep seeing each other since you have so much going on in your life. I've been concerned that you might not want to resurrect anything from the past."

"Hmm. Yes, resurrecting things from the past. That's actually correct," she said, sipping her tea.

David's face fell. "I'm sorry you feel that way." His voice was a bit shaky.

Alex smiled. "Why don't you wait until you hear me out before you jump to conclusions?"

He adjusted his six-foot frame in the seat and wrapped his fingers around the coffee cup as if to gain strength from it. "Okay, I'm listening."

"It's true I wouldn't want to re-create our old relationship. But I've been experiencing something very different with you since I got back from the mountains."

"Oh? And what is that?" asked David, leaning forward, now intrigued. He pushed his coffee cup out of the way.

"I've been letting down the walls that I had maintained so fiercely before," she said. She waited for a moment to let her words sink in. "I'm beginning to feel the value of really talking with you, sharing, and allowing myself to be vulnerable."

David was incredulous. His mouth began to drop, but he checked it. He just shook his head slowly from side to side. "I never thought I'd hear you say anything like that. I'm amazed." He took her hand in both of his. "But I'm still not clear on what's this is all about."

Alex smiled, turned over one of his hands and looked into it. "See this line?" she said, tracing one of the creases in his hand.

He nodded, smiling and curious.

"It's your heart line. Now look at this," she said, turning her own hand over and showing him a very similar line. She placed her hand over his so the two heart lines touched.

"This is what this is all about," she said, looking deeply into David's deep, blue eyes.

CHAPTER 50

With Rosie snuggled warmly between her parents, Alex found herself not wanting to sleep yet. There was much she had to think about now that she and David were together again. She and their daughter had moved into David's house since it was large and rambling, with plenty of yard for Rosie to explore. As she lay comfortably with the two people she loved most in the world, she savored the sound of birds in the trees outside their upstairs bedroom window.

She reflected on her growing feeling that her personal life was becoming a solid foundation upon which she could build the rest of her life. It was comforting and freed her mind to consider where she was going to focus her attention, particularly now that she was working practically full-time with Jim Buckingham. Every morning she was awakening with a smile on her face and an excited expectation of the day ahead. More often than not, she found herself singing in the shower, dancing in the kitchen as she fixed breakfast, or on days when David fixed breakfast, cuddling with Rosie. She found great pleasure in spending quality time with her family before Rosie went off to school and David retired to his studio in the loft. She cherished the gift of seeing them again at each day's end.

But she also found a deep feeling of expansion in her heart because of her work. Each day, the usual routines in her office were replaced more and more by important moments. She made a new habit of stopping at a flower or candy shop before riding the elevator just to buy treats for various people there. She loved surprising people now so she didn't just routinely pass out gifts to everyone. She would choose only one person every few days and try to match the color of flower to the person's personality. Or she would buy animal shaped lollipops for her coworkers' children. Ralph Billings told her often now how she had improved the work environment for everyone. His approval meant a great deal to her, but she told him he didn't need to keep telling her. She knew now that she was valued - and liked.

As she lay in bed, watching the sun begin its brightening, she thought about her recent dream in the deep pool. She had been able to appreciate the life review when she traveled through the watery halls, but had yet to understand why the suffering people were reaching out to her. She didn't understand how she could help them merely by using her hands.

Rosie muttered in her sleep and turned over, flopping her arm over David's chest. Alex saw him smile and reach out to the little girl. She was filled with love for the both of them.

As she went back to her reverie, she suddenly remembered what she had said to David at the diner when she put her hand on his. *This is what it's all about.* Her eyes widened as she realized the import of the dream's message for her to use her hands. It seemed connected somehow to love. Then, as her linear mind was struggling to discount the experience with David as mere coincidence, over her mind's eye floated the name of Jim's non-profit business that had been giving her so much joy: "Helping Hands."

Of course! That's must be what the dream message meant. Get back together with David as well as work for Jim's organization. She thought it made sense and was satisfied by the simplicity of her realization.

Being careful not to wake Rosie or David, Alex slid out of bed and went into the bathroom to shower. As she turned on the hot water and began brushing her teeth, the mirror began fogging. As she reached for a towel to wipe off the mist, she thought she saw the image of Mack and Betty. She was startled but leaned in to see more clearly. She sensed that if they were actually there, that they would be smiling at her.

She put down her toothbrush, smiled, leaned against the sink and spoke aloud. "You guys sure show up in the strangest places."

After a few minutes of reverie with the fogged mirror, she pushed herself away from the sink, dropped her nightgown on the floor and stepped into the shower. As she washed her body, she had a powerful sense that she would be seeing her two friends very soon.

As she stepped out of the shower and reached for her towel, she spied a red rose lying on the sink counter. As she reached for it, she smiled, appreciating David's grounding presence in her life.

CHAPTER 51

Alex bent down to peer into Mack's car. "Well, I got your call and here I am. Are you ready for me?" she joked.

"More than ever," said Betty, motioning for Alex to get in the back seat. "Put your bag down on the floor and get comfortable. We have a long drive ahead."

Alex did as she was told and waited expectantly for Mack to start the engine. Nothing.

A few minutes went by and no one spoke. Finally, feeling anxious, Alex asked, "What are we waiting for?"

"Oh, we thought we'd wait for your brother," Mack said, trying to keep a straight face.

In the rear view mirror, Alex saw his eyes sparkling. "Oh, I get it. Very funny. Ha, ha."

They all laughed, recalling her first introduction to Mack's and Betty's world those long months ago.

Mack turned the ignition key and soon they were rolling down the road on their way out of town.

Betty turned to look at Alex. "You did bring the quilt."

Knowing this was not meant as a question but more as a command, she nodded. She knew without having been told that the quilt was an integral part of her ever-expanding experience. She also knew it would show her where she was going.

Before leaving home, Alex had taken the quilt from the mothproof box she kept it in. Rosie was staying at a friend's house and David was submerged in a challenging design project, so she knew her family would be fine without her for a few days.

She had spread the quilt out over the bed and studied it. Somehow, she was not surprised that the colors had again become more vivid than ever and the dark spot indicating the beast had moved to the center of the pathway. She understood this to mean that she had truly grown out of and released the chaos from the early parts of her life, and she was deeply touched. Emotion coursed through her and tears streamed from her eyes. She knew only good could come from further exploration.

Now, traveling with Mack and Betty, she snuggled down into the seat, looked out of the window at the passing scenery, and enjoyed her ride.

Soon she fell asleep and didn't awaken until she felt the car come to a halt. The old engine shuddered and knocked as Mack turned it off with the key. She stretched her neck to see out the window.

"Are we there?" she asked, rubbing her eyes.

"We are, but you're not," said Betty as she opened the door and stepped out.

"Yet!" said Mack, laughing again.

"Ugh," Alex said with a mock moan. She knew she could trust her two friends, even though she also knew they were leading her into the unknown.

CHAPTER 52

"No wonder you wanted me to stow my gear in the back seat. What in the world have you got in here?" Alex asked Mack and Betty as they began unloading the items from the trunk.

"You'll see," Mack said, winking at her.

She knew enough not to question further and began helping them. As she laid down her first armload, she looked around. She could see for miles and realized they were in the desert. Somehow, she had expected they would return to the mountains, perhaps to do more work in the cave. Here, other than a few boulders strewn here and there, there was nothing that looked like a cave. She wondered what they could do here in this desolate place.

"Here, grab this tarp and lay it down on the ground over there," Betty instructed her. "Then come back and get your sleeping bag."

Alex saw Mack setting up a large tent on another tarp he had just laid down on a spot not far from the area Betty had indicated to her. She looked at the remaining equipment and didn't think she saw another tent.

"Uh, where's my tent?" she asked, hoping it was still in the trunk of the car.

"Sleeping bag only," said Mack cryptically.

"But what if it rains?" she said, with the all-too-familiar unsettling feeling in the pit of her stomach. "I'm not much of a camper."

"Sure you are," said Mack, who was busy pounding in the tent stakes. "You didn't have a tent *or* a sleeping bag when you camped out on the mountain."

"That wasn't 'camping out' - that was being *lost!*" she replied.

Alex heard Betty guffaw from an area close by where she was setting up the cooking gear.

"I'm certainly glad I provide such great entertainment for the both of you," Alex said. She continued muttering to herself on the way back to her tarp and lonely sleeping bag.

Seeing that there was nothing much more she could do after spreading out her bag, she picked up the quilt and wandered off a few hundred yards into an area that offered a panoramic view of her surroundings.

She spread out the quilt and sat down in the center of it, being careful not to sit directly on the area where the beast was roaming around.

As she looked out over the vast expanse of desert, her thoughts turned back home to Rosie and David. When she told them that she needed to be away for a while with Betty and Mack, she was surprised at how supportive they both were. In fact, they kept looking furtively at one another and encouraging her to go as soon as she liked. She had a distinct sense they shared a secret. She smiled at that thought. She loved the way David related to Rosie and what a good father he was. She also loved how Rosie didn't seem to be growing up with any of the problems that she herself had had as a child. Nor did Rosie seem to have been harmed by Alex's "mean man" who had directed her life until that fateful day she met Mack and Betty.

She sat on the quilt for a while and only realized how long she had been there when Betty called her to join them for supper. The sun was beginning to set and the horizon had become brilliant with a radiance of colors.

She picked up the quilt and let her nose lead her toward the wonderful aromas of Betty's excellent cooking. She looked forward to a great meal with the two people who had helped her save her life. She was filled with deep gratitude.

As she put a forkful of hot, delicious food into her mouth, she said, "This makes up for no tent!" They all laughed.

CHAPTER 53

"We want you to spend the day just relaxing, eating light, and getting to know the desert," said Betty, as Alex helped her wash the breakfast dishes. They had filled the wash basin with water that Mack had boiled earlier. Alex tested its temperature by putting her fingers gingerly into the basin. Finding it acceptable, she began cleaning the plates and cups with a sponge.

She nodded at Betty's instruction, trusting the older woman's role as her teacher and guide into worlds previously unknown to her. As Betty turned away from the camp table, Alex raised her eyes to look at her. Betty was middle-aged, average height and weight, and would be rather on the plain side if it were not for her sparkling dark eyes and mop of dark, wavy hair. Now, with the history she had had with Betty and her husband, Alex felt great affection for the woman. Although she knew nothing about their personal life, how they were related, whether or not they had children, where they lived, or what they did for a living, she was sure she knew them on very deep and essential levels. At times, she allowed herself to wonder if they were otherworldly in some way - aliens from another planet, or angels, or the spirit beings she had occasionally read about in metaphysical magazines. But these days, she rejected romantic notions and just accepted them at face value. She perceived them as human, but different from most people in their relationship to life. They knew how to respond to it and how to interact with it. They acted as if there was no difference, no separation, between them and anything or anyone else. And they seemed to revel in living their lives that way.

Alex secretly hoped she would learn to live hers that way too.

She finished the washing, dried the dishes and her hands, and walked over to her sleeping area. She folded the bag and sat down on it, once again looking out over the desert. In the early morning light, it looked quite different than it had the night before. She observed it with appreciation for how light could transform itself from moment to moment, but at the same time, remaining solidly present. She considered the power of the land and how ancient it must be.

The mountains in the far distance appeared gold in the morning sun and although she knew she'd never make it all the way there, she began walking toward them.

She walked for what seemed like a few hours by the changing positions of the sun. When it was directly overhead, she realized how far she had come and looked back toward her starting point. She was startled when she couldn't see the campsite. Shaken, she began to retrace her steps in the hope she would find her way back without getting lost again.

As she walked, Alex decided not to worry and instead, mused on what she had learned from Betty and Mack. She was surprised that it had been over a year now that she had known them. She felt that she had become a different person from the one who had "escaped" from the nightmare. She reflected on how she used to expend great energy on hiding from herself what she would later come to know as the unfulfilling drudgery of her life. She watched her feet take each step ahead on the soft sand and the repetitive motion took her into a gentle walking meditation.

A sense of delight filled her as she continued. She was no longer worried in the least about being lost. She knew that she knew the way. And that way was her life.

She smiled as she finally walked into camp and was not at all surprised to see Mack and Betty smiling too.

CHAPTER 54

"We want you to have a full night's sleep so we're turning in early," said Mack, clearing up the remains of their evening meal. "You have a special day ahead of you tomorrow."

"And am I to know anything about it?" Alex asked, surmising the answer.

Mack just smiled and said, "Have a good sleep." He walked away with Betty toward a large rock. Alex watched them as they settled themselves on top of it to watch the sunset. She just shrugged, knowing better than to ignore their instructions.

Alex spread out her sleeping bag and snuggled down into it. She pulled the quilt over it, and was soon fast asleep.

Groggy with deep sleep, she became aware of someone shaking her shoulder and telling her to wake up, but it was pitch dark and she felt as if she had fallen asleep only moments before.

"Wake up, sleepyhead." Betty's soft voice brought Alex to a more conscious knowledge that it was indeed still dark and she was being pulled reluctantly out of her reverie.

"But I only just fell asleep," she said, rubbing her eyes and struggling to sit up.

"Bring your jug of water and the quilt and follow us." She heard the strength of Mack's command and knew it meant not to question. She wriggled herself free of the sleeping bag, pulled on her boots, and grabbed her canteen and the quilt as she stood up.

She looked for her two friends and saw they had already begun hiking out of camp. She loped after them.

They walked for about an hour or so and as the light of dawn made things more visible, Alex saw the mountain foothills ahead of them. This was confusing since she had not seen any mountains so close to camp the day before. She decided they must have been hidden over a screen of boulders.

Soon they were moving upward, climbing over rocks and pushing scrub bushes aside. Alex found it difficult to keep the quilt from snagging on the prickly vegetation. She decided to wrap it around her waist and secure it with her belt. She tucked the water bottle into this contraption and felt freer as she walked on.

Feeling lightheaded and winded, she called out to Betty, who was walking between her and Mack. "Could we stop for a minute? I'm afraid I may black out if I don't sit down."

Without saying a word in response, Betty stopped, with an expression on her face that Alex couldn't identify. She merely nodded and Alex knew it was permission to sit, which she did immediately. She took a huge gulp of water and then hung her head down between her knees to keep herself from fainting.

When she looked up again, she saw a large ledge of rock jutting out just above her head. Betty and Mack were still standing, waiting for her. Mack caught her eye and motioned for her to stand up and follow once more. As she rose, she felt relieved that the lightheadedness had gone and she actually felt refreshed.

She plowed ahead through the brush and rocky pathway and soon found herself on top of the ledge. It was even larger than it had seemed when she observed it from below. All three of them were standing on the huge red rock, where the vista was marvelous. Alex could see for miles and the colors of the midmorning light on the distant mountains and desert were spectacular.

She became aware that Mack and Betty weren't joining in on her sightseeing. They were busy pulling things out of their packs and sweeping the surface of the rock with a leafy branch. Mack began to hum and Betty joined in, singing words Alex could not recognize. She watched as they placed large beautifully polished stones in four areas on the rock. Alex assumed they represented the four directions.

Then Betty sprinkled water from a decorated jug on all the stones, winding her way clockwise in a circle, still singing. She went around a second time, this time sprinkling a luminescent white powder as she moved, creating a circle that now encompassed Alex. She motioned Alex to spread out the quilt in the center of the circle and sit down on it. Once again, Betty moved around the circle, this time tilting her head skyward as she sang.

Next, Betty and Mack pulled two long staffs out of their packs. Mack's was a coppery color with tiny bells attached to it in various places. There were four large red feathers affixed to the top of the staff.

Betty's staff was exquisite. It was silver, with large bells and four glistening white feathers at the top. The bright sunlight made the staff appear as if it were made of water. Alex sensed a fluid quality to it as Betty moved around the circle.

Betty stopped her singing and asked Alex, "May I have permission to enter?"

Alex was unsure why the woman was asking her permission. She felt so inferior to Betty in the knowledge the woman obviously had.

"Uh, well, yes, I suppose so," she said. But when she saw the fire in Betty's eyes at her response, she knew she must answer differently. "Yes. Enter."

It was the right response, because Betty stepped into the circle. She then directed Alex to remove all her clothing. Alex hesitated, glancing nervously over to Mack, who immediately turned his back and began softly rattling his staff and chanting his wordless songs.

She began undressing and handed each piece to Betty, who dropped them onto a blanket she had brought into the circle with her. When Alex was totally unclothed, Betty reached down for the quilt and wrapped it around the younger woman and motioned for her to sit. Betty handed the bundle of clothes to Mack, who stuffed them into a pack. She put Alex's water bottle next to her on the ground, then sat cross legged face-to-face with Alex.

"Do you remember the story I told you about finding your heart?" she asked.

Alex nodded. "The priestess story."

"Yes," said Betty. "Do you remember what happened to her when the warriors came to her village?"

"They killed her," said Alex.

"By driving a stake through her heart," prompted Betty.

Now Alex was feeling anxious and worried where this line of questioning was leading. Betty reached into her shirt, pulled out a glittering dagger, and suddenly plunged it into Alex's chest.

Alex fell backward with the shock and impact of it, but Betty caught her by the wrists to keep her upright. She looked down at her chest expecting to see gushes of blood, but saw only a small scratch. It was bleeding but not profusely and was not painful.

She looked up at Betty questioningly.

"You must keep this wound open over the next three days. Allow it to bleed into the earth by the four stones," said Betty, who was loading the dagger and her other materials into her pack. "But you must not leave the circle. Don't even step outside it for a moment. If you do, your opportunity will be gone."

Alex wanted to ask, "What opportunity?" but decided against it, knowing Betty wouldn't answer. She felt a need to know if they planned to leave her here by herself, if they would be leaving food for her, if they would be within shouting distance. But she knew it was futile to attempt to pry information from them. She had experienced their ways before when they were putting her through their ceremonies.

Accepting her situation and trusting Mack and Betty at a deep place within her, Alex merely nodded and nestled deeper into the quilt.

CHAPTER 55

Alex listened as the two walked away. She strained to hear their footsteps until she could hear nothing more. Still in a state of shock, she sat for some time before moving. She numbly reached for the water and drank deeply.

Looking at the diminished water level in the bottle sent a thrill of fear through her. *Oh god, I'm not going to have enough water for three days!*

She jumped to her feet and began looking around, as if she would suddenly find a spring leaping from the rock wall behind her. Nothing. Not even a sound of distant water. Although she remembered what Betty had told her about not leaving the circle. *Oh great. Even if there was a spring, I couldn't get to it.* She had no other option but to try to conserve her remaining water.

That decision made, her mind cleared a bit and she began to make herself as much at home in her circle as possible. She walked around the inside perimeter of it and looked at the sparkling white powder which defined the circle. She stopped at each polished stone and realized they were all a different color. Considering an assumption that they represented the four directions, she decided she could discern where she was by their placement.

She walked into the center of the circle and looked up. The sun was directly overhead. *Terrific! I'll have to wait until it moves before I can tell which stone is which.*

And so she sat.

Suddenly she remembered Betty's instruction to keep the wound open and bleeding. She looked down into the quilt at her chest and saw that the blood had coagulated. She peeled off the layer of dried blood and tried to pry the cut open. It wouldn't work. She looked around and saw a bush whose branches bent into the circle. There were thorns on the bush so she broke off a twig and scratched her wound with one of the thorns. The bleeding began again.

The process made her slightly nauseous but she forced herself to rise and move to one of the stones, a yellowish one. She leaned over it and dripped her blood on it. She moved on to the next stone, which was deep burnished red, then on to next very dark stone, and finally the last one, which was pure white. She offered a few drops of blood to each stone.

Coming back to the center of the circle, she felt freer and less nervous about this adventure. She felt the heat of the midday sun warming her and decided to remove the quilt. She carefully put it on the rock, spreading it out so the sun would warm it too. She laid down on it, spreading herself as well, so she could reach for all four of the stones with her hands and her feet. She didn't know why she did this, but it felt right and she smiled as she fell into a deep sleep.

She awakened to find herself curled tightly in a ball on her side. Feeling chilled, she reached for the quilt to wrap around her. She recognized that the sun had set and it was becoming very dark. Suddenly, she became very frightened.

Why in hell did they leave me here on my own? They know I'm not an outdoors person! I could be eaten by wild animals!

The impact of what she had just considered hit her. She realized that there most likely *were* wild animals in this isolated and mountainous spot. She leaped to her feet and paced back and forth in her circle.

Why am I staying in this stupid circle? I should be finding my way back to camp instead of offering myself up to whatever wild beasts are out here!

Alex's panic was increasing when she stubbed her toe on a rock. Grabbing at it with one hand and hopping on the other foot, trying to keep the quilt around her, and cursing loudly, she lost her balance and fell, hard, back onto the rock ledge.

"Damn!" she said, beginning to cry. "Damn, damn, damn!"

Succumbing to sobs, her body shook with despair and pent-up fear.

CHAPTER 56

Alex awoke as she felt the sun on her shoulder, the only part of her body not tucked inside the quilt. She moved carefully, feeling a deep bruise on her hip where she had fallen. She sat up and inspected her body. In addition to the bruise, she found a large scrape on her toe and various scratches on almost every other part of her. She ached all over and her tongue felt like cotton. She slowly reached for her water and as she started to gulp it, remembered her vow to conserve it. She sipped at it until she felt she could feel her tongue returning to normal. She put the bottle down, making sure the top was screwed on securely.

She stood up and realized she had hoped to see Betty or Mack - or anyone. At least she expected something to have changed. But everything was just as it was the day before. Dry, deathly quiet, and hot. No, actually hotter than yesterday. She glanced forlornly at her diminishing water, then hung her head between her folded knees and sighed deeply.

Oh shit! I'm supposed to keep this thing bleeding! She remembered Betty's order and repeated her ritual of the day before, using the thorn to open the wound and leaning over each stone to offer up her blood.

This time, when she was finished, she felt no euphoria. She only felt depressed. *This time I didn't get lost - I got abandoned.*

Suddenly, she was catapulted back into her early childhood. She was in the house where her family lived. She saw her mother busily ironing. She saw herself playing alone with some blocks, occasionally looking longingly up to her mother, who never once looked back at her.

The scene faded and Alex came back to her rocky reality. The image had been simple but it filled her with such deep misery that she burst into tears once more.

The combination of emotional stress, an empty stomach, and lack of adequate water soon threw Alex into a swirl of shakiness and palpitations in her chest. Ordinarily this would have frightened her, but she found herself observing these phenomena at what seemed to be a distance. She felt as if she were beside her physical body, not inside it nor involved with its struggles. This awareness increased and she felt noticeably freer.

She began experimenting with her new bodiless state by willing herself to move from place to place. She discovered that it would happen immediately. All she had to do was think about a place and she was there. She traveled to the mountain above her with an intention to explore, primarily for water, but found only more rocky outcroppings and bushes. She explored the desert floor and again, found nothing new.

Oh well, even if I did find water, I promised I wouldn't leave this circle. She sighed and continued her exploration.

It occurred to her that perhaps she could "fly" to regions in worlds other than the one she was in at the moment. Instantly, she found herself traveling in a multicolored realm of enormous scope and potential. She sensed she could create anything she wished here. She made balls of light with her etheric hands, huge chunks of color, rivers of gold and silver. It delighted her and she laughed aloud.

The sound of her laughter pulled her back down into her body. But it was a pleasant fall. She even enjoyed feeling her bruises and aches again because she was no longer afraid or depressed.

She felt a new power she had never felt before.

CHAPTER 57

As the day wore on, Alex's body became increasingly weak. Her hunger had faded as well as her thirst. She had to keep reminding herself to drink. It took great effort to raise the bottle to her mouth and great concentration to remember not to drink it all. Toward the end of the afternoon, her eyes were not focusing normally and she was hearing strange sounds. She even thought she heard voices, but couldn't make out what they were saying or from where they were emanating.

She alternated between sitting, wrapped in the quilt as if comatose, and stumbling around the circle. Mostly, she just stared out into the distant desert. When she would remember her task to keep the wound open she couldn't remember if she had already done it. So she anointed the stones with her blood several times.

As she finished her ritual, she rose shakily from the final stone. From the corner of her eye, she thought she saw movement. Whirling around to see what it was made her giddy. She dropped to the ground and waited for her head to clear. The sounds around her were becoming more distinct now and her heart began beating hard when she heard the sounds of wolves howling.

No, no, it can't be wolves. It's got to be just coyotes.
They won't harm me. They're probably miles away.

Heart pounding and frightened in spite of her try at
reassuring herself, she pulled herself up to a standing
position. But she was suddenly wracked with nausea. Her
head spun again and she barely made it to the edge of the
circle before she vomited. On her knees, she wiped her
mouth with the heel of her hand, then crawled weakly back
to the center of the circle. She didn't know how she knew
she had to be sick outside the circle's boundary, and was
only vaguely aware that something beside her ordinary self
was guiding her actions.

The warmth of the day still radiated from the rock
she sat upon and it calmed her and settled her stomach.
She threw off the quilt and sat, naked, not knowing
whether to cry or laugh. She felt on the edge of hysteria and
was fascinated by her acceptance of it.

She glanced down at the quilt and saw that she was
sitting near the dark shape. She watched, intrigued,
through her with blurred vision, as the beast moved along
the pathway. Suddenly he stopped, looked up at her, and
motioned for her to follow him. Without reasoning it out,
she silently assented and instantly found herself walking
alongside him on the quilted trail.

She knew she was traveling through the middle
section of the quilt and felt as if it were known territory.
Her expanded state of awareness, due to the stresses on
her body and mind, offered her unique perceptions. Cacti
and rocks became living, moving creatures. Lizards and
jackrabbits transformed into strange, geometric shapes.
Psychedelic colors moved sinuously across the sky, turning
clouds into faces that called to her.

Alex was fascinated by what she was seeing. Once
again, freed from the restraints of her weakened body, she
was able to move over the quilt's terrain with ease. She was

194

thoroughly enjoying her act of surrender to these new experiences.

Suddenly, the beast growled at her for attention. He thrust out a hairy paw in front of her to stop her from going any further. She saw an enormous, golden gate that reached skyward and seemed to encompass her entire field of vision. It was ornate, with incredible filigree designs and carvings of otherworldly creatures. Awed by its beauty, she reached out to touch it.

As her fingers made contact with the golden metal, a shock coursed through her, forcing her head to be thrown backward. She found herself floating supine upward until she was about seven feet in the air.

"Are you ready?" boomed a powerful voice.

Thinking she was being asked if she was ready to enter the beautiful gate, she smiled and nodded.

CHAPTER 58

Abruptly, she dropped from her celestial perch down, down, down for what seemed to be miles through a dark tunnel. She landed with a thud on cold ground.

Realizing she was back on her rocky ledge, she felt deeply disappointed. She had so longed for entrance to what she imagined would be a new existence, one without struggle or difficulty. In the back of her mind, she held the hope that one day, some sort of perfect, heavenly reality would replace all adversity in her life.

Alex wrapped the quilt around her, shaking her head to clear it but the motion only stirred more stupefaction. She groggily reached for her water bottle, took a gulp and put it down again beside her.

She could hardly keep her eyes open but was aware that night had fallen. She couldn't make sense out of how many nights she had spent on the ledge so far. In her state of mind, it felt as if she'd been there only moments as well as for years. She tried using logic to determine how long it was since Betty and Mack left.

As the thought of them entered her mind, she saw them standing outside the circle.

"Hey! You're back! I knew you wouldn't abandon me!" she shouted, struggling to her feet. She staggered toward them and fell, just inside the boundary. As she pulled herself up, she looked up, expecting to see their faces. But there was no one there. There was no sound. No reassuring voice. Nothing except the wind ruffling the dry branches in the brush.

Alex began to wail, rocking back and forth on her heels, slapping at her head. "Why have you abandoned me? Why?" she demanded, believing she was directing her complaint at Betty and Mack.

Suddenly, the face of her father appeared, hovering a few feet from her. "I didn't mean to hurt you," he said.

Jarred to the core, Alex bolted upright, sitting back on her haunches. "What?" she demanded angrily.

"I didn't want to leave. It was just that your mother didn't want me around you anymore," he said, tears in his eyes.

"Why would she want that?" Alex felt her heart pounding in her chest. She was also vaguely aware that the wound had reopened on its own and was bleeding slowly. She looked down for a moment and touched the blood with her fingers.

She dumbly looked at her father again, holding out her stained fingers as if they held a question.

His tears continued to flow. "Because she knew I loved you more than I loved her."

Swift thoughts began filling her mind. She finally understood, after years of painful wondering, why her mother had never shown her any affection. She knew in her heart why the woman had only attended to the necessities for survival and not to her.

"Now that you understand, it's time to forgive her," said her father.

"How can I forgive her for not loving me? How can I forgive her for taking you away from me?"

"It was all meant to be."

198

"Meant to be?" Alex said. "When would it be right for a child not to have the love and support of her parents?" Anger was rising fiercely within her.

"When that child's Soul chose parents who would push her to find herself, to learn to be strong and courageous on her own. When that child's Soul - your Soul - had developed to the place where it could learn to fly by itself."

Her father was smiling now.

As she started to complain again, a strange calm came over her. Just as she had experienced the review of her life in the tunnel some time ago, now her life passed before her eyes again. But this time it seemed to be from a higher, far more expansive prospective.

As the understanding grew, Alex was aware that something, a strong presence, was entering her entire being. She felt it connecting to her physical body, but other indefinable parts of her as well. There was a warm and effervescent quality to it and its essence filled her entire being. She couldn't tell how long the feeling lasted, but when it faded, she felt deeply disappointed.

She opened her eyes and was surprised that it was daylight. She no longer felt dizzy or weak. In fact, she was energized and felt jubilant for reasons she couldn't understand. She simply basked in the joy of it.

She stood, and as the quilt dropped to the ground at her feet, she noticed its top section. She leaned forward to get a better look and saw the beast, now grinning up at her.

He was inside the golden gate.

CHAPTER 59

Alex checked her wound to make sure it was still open. She did her stone ritual, sipped her water conservatively, and spent the rest of the early morning lying naked in the sun on the quilt.

She watched fluffy white clouds scutter through the sky and birds swoop overhead. She wondered what they were, and guessed they must be hawks of some kind. There were other birds, large and black, that she particularly liked. They seemed sassy and confident. She laughed when one of them paused to spend a few moments sitting on an overhanging rock some twenty or so yards up the mountain from her. He persisted in staring at her as if he had never seen something so interesting.

As the raven flew away, Alex took another sip of water and crooked her elbows behind her and reclined against them. But feeling incredibly happy about the visit from her father, she neglected to replace the cap securely.

As she pushed the bottle a little ways from her where she sat, she set a strong intention to contact her father when she got home. She no longer cared if her mother knew if she developed a relationship with him. She would handle her mother just fine. She felt freer than ever from the old pressure to conform to her mother's rules and expectations. She knew she could hold her own with the woman now. And she knew the reason why. She was becoming her authentic self, no longer controlled by her mother's fears. She was sure, as she had suspected weeks ago, that now she could allow her mother to be just who she was without being upset by it. And while she knew she would not be choosing to spend much time with her, when she did, it would be a far different experience than in the past.

The past. She mused upon the significance of no longer living her life based upon it. She wondered what changes were in store for her and although most of her life had been based upon fear of change before, now she felt a deep welcoming of it within her. She thought of how her body changed as she grew up and how it now made perfect sense that her mind and emotions must do so similarly. She thought about how crippling it would be to try to hold the body from growing. This thought helped her see how she had crippled her feeling nature by trying to control changes when they appeared in her life. She fully understood now how she had closed herself off from David and the love in their relationship because she had been afraid of change. At the end of the honeymoon stage of their marriage, she had distanced herself from him in hopes of preventing anything from changing. She saw clearly now how that had backfired and created the very thing she feared the most. She had actually killed any last vestiges of the honeymoon. She had cut off any potential for further love to grow between them. Seeing this at that time as a problem of David's, she felt justified in leaving him.

A smile grew as Alex felt the warmth of more than the sun. It was the warmth of love, renewed and made real by the opening of her heart.

CHAPTER 60

Alex felt full and satisfied, although certainly not with food or physical comfort. Night was once again drawing near and it was several degrees colder than the previous evenings. She pulled the quilt closer around her and gazed at the stars and the exquisitely large full moon. She had never seen it so huge. She joked with herself that it had grown just for her.

Thirsty, she felt around her for her water bottle. As her fingers found it, her heart sank. It was lying on its side, empty. When she forgot earlier to replace the cap, then bumped it without seeing what she did, the water had drained out. Feeling panicky, she tried to think of how much longer she would be on the rock ledge. She thought that she remembered Betty or Mack saying something about three days, but now she was unsure of what they actually had said as well as how many days she'd been there by herself. As her panic grew, she began pacing around the circle again.

Something drew her attention to the four stones. She stopped the frantic pacing and looked. They seemed to shine brightly in the moonlight and seemed to be encouraging her to pray.

She asked sincerely and strongly for help in getting through this ordeal. At the end of her prayers, she felt relieved of fear and sat watching the moon. Soon her body released into a reclining position and she slept.

Alex was awakened by the loud howling of wolves. She knew they were close by. She was so frightened she couldn't move. She was lying on her back with her legs and arms reaching for the stones again. She was stunned by this posture because it seemed being curled into a ball might offer the best protection.

Suddenly, they were upon her, ripping and tearing at her. In shock, her consciousness lifted out of her body and watched as they tore her to pieces. She observed in a sort of resigned horror as two wolves carried her legs off in one direction while two others took her arms in another. One particularly large wolf wrenched her head from her body and ran off in a new direction with it.

By now, she was in a state of absolute disbelief, feeling it was happening to someone else, not to her. But when she looked back at the last wolf, a large white one, she recognized what it held in its mouth. It was her heart. It stood looking at her for several moments before loping away.

Alex moaned in her sleep. She was vaguely aware that she was fighting to pull herself into a fetal position but could not. She felt paralyzed. She struggled to pull herself out of sleep but merely sunk back more deeply than before.

Betty was standing just outside the circle and was holding a large pack. She opened it, reached in and pulled out Alex' arms and legs, placing them in their right positions on the quilt. Next, she lifted out Alex' head and placed it gently next to the torso.

Finally, she reverently pulled the heart, still beating, from the bag and let it slide back into Alex' chest.

Betty began her lovely song, softly chanting and moving gently around the circle. With the song's call, Alex became more aware and awake until she was able to sit and then stand.

She was naked and was aware of Mack's presence behind her but she didn't care if he saw her bareness. It seemed perfectly natural.

She stood calmly waiting. For what, she didn't know.

Then Betty stopped in front of her and motioned for her to look down at her chest.

Alex saw a glittering gold dagger protruding from her heart. Strangely, it didn't cause any discomfort.

She looked at Betty, remembering the story of the priestess. She recalled that the Great Mother had told her that she must keep the spear in her heart.

"Just pull it out," said Betty.

"What? I don't understand. I thought it had to stay there."

"Just pull it out."

Confused, but trusting Betty, Alex tugged at the dagger. At first it resisted but then released and slid out, bloodless, in her hand. As if made of spun sugar, it began dissolving until it was gone, except for a slight glow in her hand.

Alex looked at the wound and was amazed to see it healing itself quickly until nothing remained except a small, ragged scar that, to her, looked strangely like the shape of the beast.

CHAPTER 61

"This is the most delicious breakfast I've ever had in my life!" Alex was shoveling pancakes and potatoes into her mouth alternately with huge gulps of water. "I don't think I'll ever get my fill of this stuff." She pointed to her cup.

"Not so fast or you'll lose it," warned Mack. He was just sitting on his haunches watching her. Betty was nearby, folding up blankets and breaking down their tent.

"I wouldn't even care," said Alex, wiping her mouth with a napkin. "I am totally confident that there's more where that came from!"

All three laughed.

The day was beautiful. The sky was filled with fluffy clouds and was bright blue already in the early morning hours. The mountain peaks in the distance were shades of purple and red in the dawn light. A little brown bird was pecking around the campsite in its hunt for something delicious.

"When you're finished there, let's finish packing. We have a long drive back," said Betty. Then she looked at Alex, smiling mysteriously. "But before we leave, there's something I want to give you."

They all got to work clearing up the breakfast dishes and putting all the camp supplies in the trunk. Alex folded the quilt carefully and placed it on the back seat.

Mack walked away from camp into a stand of bushes to do what Alex guessed were his morning ablutions. She chuckled at his need for privacy when she had bared it all for him the night before. Or at least she thought she had.

Shrugging her shoulders, she scanned the campsite for any missed articles. Betty called to her from a group of boulders nearby.

Alex joined her, looking at her expectantly.

Betty laughed at her expression. "I'm glad you haven't lost your innocence," she said, patting Alex's cheek.

Alex flushed.

"Now that you know who you are, I want to ask you about your name," said Betty with a penetrating look.

"My name?"

"Yes. What is your name?"

"Uh, Alex, of course," she said, nervously grasping at her thighs with her hands.

"Not really," said Betty. "Do you know what your name means?"

"Well, my mother once told me she named me for someone in a film she liked."

"But what does it mean?" Betty persisted.

"I really don't know. Alex. No, nothing comes to mind."

"But it's not really Alex, is it?" Betty said, more as a statement than a question.

Alex' face reddened. "Oh. Well. If you mean Alexandra. I never liked it so I changed it to Alex."

"You didn't like it because you weren't ready for it," said Betty.

Alex was confused. "What do you mean, ready for it?"

"Alexandra is the perfect name for you because it means 'helper and defender of humankind.'"

Alex was stunned. "I never knew that. But I'm not sure that I'm ready to take that on, even now."

Betty just smiled. "You'll see. And in the meantime, I have this to give you." She pulled a small velvet bag out of her pocket. From it she pulled a large pendant that was hanging on a gold chain.

She placed the necklace over Alex' head and adjusted the pendant so that it rested on her heart. Alex looked down at it and realized it was a beautiful rendering of the quilt, in exquisite detail. In its center was the beast holding a dagger in one hand and a heart in the other.

CHAPTER 62

"And then what did you do, Mom, when you spilled your water?" Rosie was sitting close to Alex, holding the quilt cozily around her shoulders. Since Alex returned home, the little girl loved hearing the stories about the quilt over and over again and was spellbound by her mother's latest and carefully edited tale of adventure. Alex planned to tell David the complete story but only that night after Rosie was asleep.

"Well, I just prayed, Sweetie Pie," she said, stroking Rosie's curly brown hair. "Just like we're going to do tonight before you go to bed."

"What will that do? I didn't spill anything," said Rosie, in all her innocent glory.

Alex laughed and reassured her. "It's just a good thing to do. It helps us be happy."

"Oh, Mom," said Rosie, giggling and chucking Alex's chin with her sweet fingers. "I'm already happy! You're here and Daddy's here."

Then the little girl paused thoughtfully. She frowned and said, "But I think I'd be even happier if I could have a pet!" She brightened, looking hopefully at Alex.

Laughing, Alex hugged Rosie.

"That sounds like a great idea but we'll have to check with your dad first."

David was just rounding the corner from the kitchen, carrying a huge bowl of hot popcorn and balancing a tray of drinks.

"What's such a great idea?" he asked.

Rosie leapt off the couch and jumped around gleefully, throwing her head back and howling, singing, "I'm going to have a dog! I'm going to have a dog!"

As she galloped around the living room, Alex looked at David and realized the secret he and Rosie had lately been keeping.

He grinned sheepishly at her and tossed some popcorn into his mouth.

CHAPTER 63

Weeks flew by in an endless parade of new projects inspired by the success of Buckingham Industries' community activities. Nowadays, Alex had to expand her focus to include other businesses that wanted to duplicate Buckingham's accomplishments. They had seen how profitable community service could ultimately be for both the fiscal side of business as well as for public goodwill. She enjoyed watching corporate types in their grey flannels opening up to new ideas that stimulated and contributed to the joy and well-being that their charitable activities could offer people.

But no matter how busy she became, she always had time to retrieve Rosie from school, spend quality time with David, and even take occasional solo hikes in the hills. She did this to keep fresh her experiences with Betty and Mack.

These days she didn't see them much but she knew they tended to show up without notice.

She and Tam worked together closely in the garden, with him sharing some of his horticultural secrets with her. She was surprised at her growing love of working with the soil and sensed it had something to do with what Mack and Betty had taught her about using her hands.

She also suspected that Tam always spoke to her in metaphorical terms because he was not really teaching her how to grow bigger artichokes. She knew, deep down, that she was being prepared for whatever her next big step would turn out to be.

On weekends, she, David, and Rosie worked with Tam in the garden. Alex found deep satisfaction in watching him talk intimately with her daughter. She knew Rosie would benefit greatly, merely by his presence.

Eileen was doing very well as Alex's Administrative Assistant. In fact, she had blossomed into quite a clever asset to the firm. Alex knew she wouldn't be working there for much longer, so was comforted in knowing Eileen could easily slip into her spot at an executive level.

Each time she thought about this, Alex felt a glow in her heart and was amazed at the thrill of new life within her body. She hadn't yet gotten over David's outrageous response when she made her announcement. He had swept her up into his arms, and called for Rosie to drop what she was doing and come with them. He carried Alex out of their apartment, plopped her and Rosie into the car, and whisked them all off to their favorite restaurant.

When they arrived, David mysteriously disappeared, but not before asking her to get them a good table. She suspected he had gone to buy her flowers.

But the most satisfying, if not surprising, moment of that evening came when the maitre de asked her for a name.

"Alex," she began, then hesitated. She pulled herself up to her full height, looked the maitre de in the eye and gloriously announced:

"Alexandra!"

ABOUT THE AUTHOR

Nanci Shanderá, Ph.D. is a spiritual teacher at EarthSpirit Center for the Transformational Arts in Northern California. She has taught in public school as well as in community colleges, hospitals, and metaphysical seminaries. As a Religious Science minister, she administered Ernest Holmes College School of Ministry in Los Angeles for many years, where she also taught transformational intensives. She has two daughters and three grandchildren.

Writing credits include several articles in spiritually based magazines, such as *The Science of Mind* and *Shaman's Drum*. Her book, *Your Inner Gold: Transform Your Life and Discover Your Soul's Purpose*, will be released by Llewellyn Publishing in June of 2013.

For a current calendar of events or to contact her regarding sponsoring workshops, lectures or book signings, she may be contacted at www.EarthSpiritCenter.com. She welcomes readers' responses, especially regarding their own experiences of transformation.